I0822805

Psychic Abilities

Unlocking Your Inner Medium and Ability for Divination, Telepathy, Astral Projection, Connecting with Spirit Guides, and Clairvoyance

Free Bonus from Silvia Hill available for limited time

Hi Spirituality Lovers!

My name is Silvia Hill, and first off, I want to THANK YOU for reading my book.

Now you have a chance to join my exclusive spirituality email list so you can get the ebooks below for free as well as the potential to get more spirituality ebooks for free! Simply click the link below to join.

P.S. Remember that it's 100% free to join the list.

~~$27~~ **FREE BONUSES**

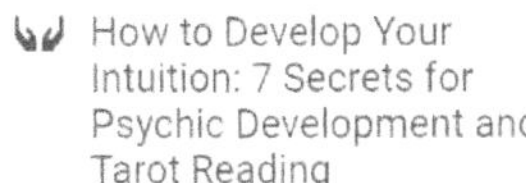

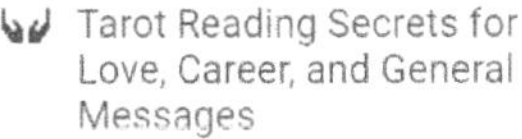

Access your free bonuses here

https://livetolearn.lpages.co/psychic-abilities-paperbck/

Table of Contents

Introduction

While the existence of psychic abilities is still a much-debated topic, there are countless examples of people being able to hear, see, sense, or perceive information no one else can. So, one of the first steps toward unlocking your potential psychic skills is dissociating the spiritual concept from how mediumship is portrayed through mainstream channels. Working on your psychic abilities is a highly spiritual practice. While doing this, you'll rely on your intuition to set you on the right path. The journey toward discovering one's inherent spiritual gift is different for everyone, as each psychic has a unique combination of cultural and religious background and personality traits.

Psychics experience extrasensory stimuli on different spiritual, mental, and physical levels. For that reason, there is a broad spectrum of extrasensory abilities that people can experience. This book will introduce you to the clairs - the four fundamental powers physics often relies on. They include skills such as seeing, hearing, and feeling the messages one receives or simply knowing it in their mind without realizing how it got there. These abilities allow psychics to peek into the future and learn to elevate themselves spiritually.

Divination can be done with or without any specific tool. However, the latter helps psychics communicate with spirits and guide them when they need information or insights about the future. You'll also learn about telepathy and astral projection - two skills linked to the *aura*. Auras are a unique form of energy that people with extrasensory gifts can only perceive.

When it comes to spiritual communication in general, this practice must be approached carefully and with great precaution. Apart from benevolent spirits and guides, you may rely on for helpful information, you'll also encounter some not-so-friendly spirits. This book offers plenty of practical advice on protecting yourself against them and cleaning yourself or anything else they might have tainted with their influence. If this doesn't work and these forces still manage to get their hold on you or someone else, you can also resort to the psychic healing techniques you'll learn about in this book. These will also work to spruce you up when psychic work drains your mental and physical energy.

Although many psychics develop their abilities during childhood, these often become buried under a mountain of conditioned beliefs. Being told that sensitivity to stimuli no one else experiences isn't a good thing can make anyone feel disconnected from their psychic gifts. Not to mention the stress and expectations of daily life. Fortunately, this doesn't have to mean that you'll lose your abilities. And even if you haven't felt them beforehand, they might still be there, lying dormant and waiting for you to awaken them.

Through the numerous examples of how others have discovered their powers and user-friendly techniques you can use to find your own, this book will guide you through this challenging yet incredibly rewarding journey. Now, to unlock your inner medium, you'll need to arm yourself with patience. Your powers will not appear magically overnight, nor will they start to develop when you finally reveal them. To elevate them to the highest level, you'll need to continuously practice and keep honing your intuition. So, if you're prepared to embark on this journey, by all means, let's delve right into it!

Chapter 1: Are You Ready for Psychic Abilities?

Perception is a very powerful thing. Imagine this: You're sitting with your friends, and one of them leans into you and says, "something is wrong with Shelly; she isn't acting like herself." You take a look at Shelly, but she's acting normal. Not long after, Shelly's facial expressions change, and she breaks down in tears, saying, "I am not okay, and I can't hold it in any longer." You look at your friend in disbelief and wonder whether she's a psychic or if she's just more perceptive than you.

Being a psychic is generally described as having the ability to perceive all types of sensory data spiritually, physically, and emotionally.

https://www.pexels.com/photo/white-moon-on-hands-3278643/

This opening chapter will help you grasp the fundamentals of psychic abilities, what they are and feel like, and the beliefs and science behind them. Thanks to a quick and self-informative quiz, you'll also find out whether you're a psychic yourself.

Understanding Psychic Abilities

Being a psychic is generally described as having the ability to perceive all types of sensory data spiritually, physically, and emotionally. In most cases, this ability starts in early childhood. A parent or grandparent may have passed down this gift to you, or you may have grown up in an environment that enabled you to develop and nurture this ability.

Not everyone with psychic abilities is aware that they possess this gift. Like in the previous example, they may think they are just perceptive - or empaths. Some people try to force their intuition to see whether they are indeed psychics. However, this is something you can't force; in most cases, your abilities will come out naturally. For instance, you're relaxing with a glass of wine or taking a shower. Suddenly, you find the solution to a problem you've been struggling with or figure out something about someone you haven't noticed before. This may be a sign that you are a psychic, which you may not immediately be ready to accept, blaming your spur of enlightenment on the booze instead. That said, this information came to you somewhere - it could very well be your psychic abilities unveiling themselves to you.

Psychic abilities allow you to see and feel things about others that most people can't. Psychics often experience synesthesia, where two of your senses overlap due to external stimuli. For instance, you may see shapes when listening to music or hear a specific sound when smelling something, or in the case of a psychic, you begin associating a color or shape with a person. You may think something is wrong with you if you see a color around someone, but what you see is their aura.

People with psychic abilities can sense something isn't right, unable to explain why or how they have this feeling. For instance, your friend invites you to dinner at a well-known restaurant, but you suggest another one instead because, deep down, you feel uneasy about that particular venue. Later that evening, you learn that a fire broke out at that restaurant on the same night you were supposed to have dinner there. You probably think this was just a coincidence, but chances are it was your gut feeling warning you. While most people have a gut feeling, a psychic's intuition is more powerful than anyone else's and can even save their life.

If you possess psychic abilities, your dreams can even help guide you toward something or send you a specific message. Some dreams can be vivid or seem like visions that are so powerful that you can't ignore them. For instance, your deceased brother comes to you in a dream to tell you to call his wife. You call her and find out she's going through something and could use your help. Similarly, your psychic ability may also show in the form of a daydream. For instance, you are taking a shower and see an image of money. Upon arriving at work, your boss informs you that everyone will get a bonus this quarter as a thank-you for the team's hard work. You may also think of someone from high school and then run into them later that day or read a message from them the following day.

Everyone experiences a wide range of emotions daily. However, psychics tend to experience strong ones without an apparent, rational explanation. For instance, you may have the urge to cry for no reason, then later receive news from your sister that your cousin has just passed away. None of these are coincidences, especially if they are recurring incidences. While it's easy to dismiss these as pure fantasies, opening your eyes and being willing to accept your "extraordinary" abilities can enable you to tap into your psychic potential.

There is a common element in all these examples and situations: feeling or seeing something before it happens. Most people attribute this to having a sixth sense – it can help you pick up on supernatural signals and perceive things that other people aren't aware of.

Psychic Abilities and Extrasensory Perception

People naturally depend on their five senses to perceive and understand everything going on around them. However, everyone has a sixth sense that they rarely pay attention to Extrasensory perception (ESP). Many people consider it to be the same thing as intuition is a gift that can only be developed through the use of your sixth sense. Your sixth sense will allow you to perceive things beyond your five senses, hence the extrasensory name perception.

Extrasensory perception often manifests as a strange, uneasy feeling you experience before something bad happens. Because your body is made up of energy, the sixth sense is the perfect tool to respond to other people's energy. For instance, you arrive at the office only to feel inexplicably uncomfortable, as if something just went down. You discover that one of your co-workers was just laid off. You haven't seen your co-worker, heard gossip, or even whispers. You have simply picked up on the energy in the room using your sixth sense.

The sixth sense is the inner voice that makes you aware of things that can't be perceived with your other senses. It's this feeling inside of you that just "knows something," such as if someone is trustworthy or not at first glance. You can experience the sixth sense in various ways, like feeling something in your body, hearing a voice, seeing a vision, smelling something, tasting something bad in your mouth, or simply knowing.

Using your psychic ability implies tapping into your sixth sense or ESP to see, hear, or feel things that may not be obvious to your other senses. So, to develop psychic abilities, you must be attuned to your sixth sense and understand that what your gut feeling is telling you isn't a coincidence or something that you should dismiss. You can't be a psychic if you don't fully utilize and rely on your sixth sense.

People with Psychic Abilities

The word "psychic" has been thrown around a lot lately. Some people dismiss it because they can't comprehend that such power truly exists, whereas others can attest to these abilities as they have experienced them firsthand. Certain people are reluctant to believe in these abilities because history hasn't been kind to psychics, to say the least. According to a psychic medium and author, Bernadette Gold, who grew up in the 1960s, it was a hard time for psychics as people struggled to understand or embrace those with this unique gift. As a result, it took her decades to realize that she was an empath and had psychic abilities.

Nowadays, people have grown more tolerant and accepting, and more and more people are encouraged to be their truest selves. If you suspect you have this unique ability, you should embrace it. You probably wonder how you can tell whether you have this gift. The examples mentioned above may give you a clue. However, reading about people who experience psychic abilities firsthand can give you a better idea of what this gift feels like.

There is a story about a woman who saw a vision of her mother's friend's house ravaged by a storm. The vision was so vivid that she even saw the faces of everyone who lived under that roof. The very next day, a hurricane hit the area where her mother's friend lived. While the woman didn't think there was anything to her vision, she admits that she usually experiences an odd feeling before something bad happens.

A woman and her husband wanted to have a child. The woman was depressed for years because they weren't able to conceive. One day, she went on a hike and saw a clear image of a little boy. She saw every detail of his face, what he was wearing, the color of his eyes and hair. It was as if he was truly there. Two years later, she gave birth to a boy who was the spitting image of the kid she was in her vision.

Another person tells a story about driving his friend to the airport. As he was getting in his car, something inside told him not to leave the airport. So, he decided to stay in his car for half an hour in case his friend missed his plane. He claims he just couldn't bring himself to leave. A few minutes later, a powerful earthquake hit. Cars were shaking, and people were frantically fleeing the airport. His distraught friend called him, asking if he could come and pick him up. He told him that, luckily, he was still there. He admitted to having experienced this feeling on various occasions before, with his gut telling him to do or not do something.

People with this ability say it's easy for them to pick up on things in their surroundings that most people don't notice. They also often get premonitions about themselves or their families; sometimes, a sudden vision or voice can serve as a lifesaving warning. They are highly sensitive to what goes on around them. They are also empathetic individuals who can sense other people's emotions even when they attempt to mask their feelings. Some say they can learn personal information about others by getting visuals when they are around them. People with this ability also say it comes naturally to them, just like using their other senses. After all, no one thinks before they hear or smell something - the same applies to using your sixth sense.

The Science behind Psychic Abilities

You may be surprised to learn that the U.S. government has conducted various research and experiments on the topic of psychic abilities. These experiments aimed to learn about psychic spying and prove that people can have paranormal abilities. Academic experts have reviewed this secret government research and concluded that having paranormal abilities isn't a farce, contrary to what many people have been claiming.

According to California University professor Jessica Utts, it has been scientifically proven that having psychic abilities is possible. She added that since we now know these abilities are real, there is no need for further research. It's best to use these resources to understand how these abilities work. Oregon University psychology professor Ray Hyman agrees with Utts that things now seem more hopeful than ever regarding the topic of psychic abilities.

Psychologist William McDougall and founder of parapsychology J. B. Rhine also conducted their own experiments to prove that people can have psychic abilities. They used cards with specific symbols and asked participants to guess the card being held. Chance also played a role in this experiment, as some people simply guessed instead of knowing which card it was. However, researchers are still using this experiment and letting statistics be the main determinant. This experiment typically involves 25 distinct cards. If someone guesses five cards, they may be just lucky. However, if they guess 15 or 20 cards, this can reduce the likelihood of chance as a primary factor, showing that these individuals may use their psychic abilities. Researchers use statistics to determine whether the participants are using their psychic abilities or simply guessing.

The Rhine also improved his research by using dice instead of cards. The results showed that some people could use their psychic abilities to guess the dice correctly, and the results were very positive. Participants could use their abilities when the experiments were conducted in a controlled environment.

Despite persisting doubts and general defiance toward anything out of the ordinary, scientific research has shown that people can indeed possess psychic abilities.

Can Anyone Have Psychic Abilities?

Yes, anyone can nurture this skill and develop psychic abilities. We all possess a sixth sense, even if we don't use it or aren't even aware that we have it. Since having psychic abilities mainly depends on using your sixth sense, anyone can have this gift - tapping into your sixth sense and using it can help you unlock this special gift. You must start believing in yourself and paying attention to your intuition and what it's trying to tell you. Don't ignore or dismiss the things you see, feel, or hear. Your sixth sense is here for a reason, often to guide or protect you; it's the gateway to unlocking and sharpening your psychic abilities.

Quiz

Now that you've learned about psychic abilities, you probably wonder if you possess this gift. You may already have psychic abilities but aren't aware of them. This simple "true" or "false" quiz will answer the question you have been pondering: Do I already have latent psychic abilities?

Check "True" to the statements that apply to you and "False" to the ones that don't.

1. **Your gut feeling often warns you about things that later turn out to be true.**
   - True
   - False
2. **You often experience déjà vu.**
   - True
   - False
3. **You often see lights or colors around living things.**
   - True
   - False
4. **You have visions or flashes of certain events before they occur.**
   - True
   - False
5. **You have vivid dreams that provide guidance, a warning, or reveal certain information.**
   - True
   - False
6. **You experience strong emotions like grief, joy, fear, or excitement inexplicably, only for an incident to happen later and explain these emotions.**
   - True
   - False

7. **You can tell when someone is deceiving you or lying to you.**
   - True
   - False
8. **You often get a positive or negative feeling from a particular place.**
   - True
   - False
9. **You have family members who have psychic abilities.**
   - True
   - False
10. **External stimuli can easily overwhelm you.**
    - True
    - False
11. **You sometimes simply know things with no rational reason for how you got this information.**
    - True
    - False

If your answers are overwhelmingly true, there's a chance that you are a psychic. However, if you answer mostly false, there is no need to fret. You may simply need to figure out how to tap into your abilities and unlock your gift, which you will learn more about later in the book.

Explanation

To help clarify things, let's explain the prompts in this quiz and what each one aims to check.

Gut Feeling

A gut feeling strongly resembles intuition. However, the main difference is that you can also experience a sensation in your body, which generally doesn't happen with intuition. It's usually a feeling that you know something. For instance, you get goosebumps when you enter a particular place or feel strangely uneasy when you meet a certain person. This is your gut feeling telling you that something isn't right.

Déjà Vu

Déjà vu is a French term that means "already seen." It's a feeling you get during an event or situation that something is very familiar or that you've experienced it before - when *you know that you haven't.* For instance, you go to a restaurant for the first time, and as you take a seat, you get this feeling that you've been there before. While you know this is the first time you have visited this restaurant, or it has just opened, you still can't shake this feeling.

Lights or Colors

The light and colors you see around people are called *auras.* An aura is an invisible energy field that radiates from all living things; its energy is often spiritual, and only a person with psychic abilities can see or feel it. The color of a person's aura can reveal a great deal about them and their emotions. An aura is similar to a "vibe," so when you react to someone's vibe, whether positively or negatively, you are most likely feeling their aura.

Visions or Flashes

This statement checks whether you've ever experienced premonitions.

Vivid Dreams

Some people struggle to learn the difference between a vivid dream and a regular one. In short, vivid dreams feel more "real" than regular dreams. They're so intense that you won't be able to forget or ignore them. If you wake up and your dream feels like something that happened in your real life and lingers in your memory, then this dream is trying to tell you something.

Strong Emotions

This statement checks whether you're able to feel something before it occurs.

Spotting Liars

This statement aims to see how perceptive you are when spotting liars.

A Place's Vibe

Sometimes, a place has a strange vibe or is filled with negative people, making you feel uneasy.

Family Members

Relatives often pass down psychic abilities. If one of your parents or grandparents has this gift, you may also have it.

External Stimuli

Psychics tend to be more sensitive to external stimuli than most people.

Knowing

When your sixth sense makes you aware of something, you just know that this information is true, even if you don't have evidence to support it.

Ultimately, anyone can be a psychic. Every person is born with a sixth sense, but as they grow up, they rely on the logical part of their brains and often neglect this gift they have. In parallel, others nurture and develop this sense, opening the door to a world of possibilities and things you never knew were there. Your sixth sense is waiting for you to tap into it so you can explore the psychic world and everything it has to offer. Regardless of your personality type or spiritual goals, becoming a psychic is a process that requires patience and dedication. Now that we've covered the basics, it's time to delve deeper into the realm of psychic powers.

Chapter 2: The Clairs I. Supernatural Seeing and Hearing

Have you ever walked through the woods and sensed something was about to happen? Maybe you heard a twig snap or a bird fly away just before something started creeping toward you. That sixth sense, –or Clairvoyance, is your ability to sense and understand things beyond what your five senses can detect. The idea of having a "sixth sense" has fascinated people for centuries. The ability to perceive things beyond our basic senses would be a truly remarkable and useful skill, especially in this digital age when we are constantly bombarded with information. Culturally, we seem to be moving away from focusing on our sensory experiences and more toward virtual experiences in the form of virtual reality, video games, apps, etc. In response, many people are developing Clair abilities as a way to reconnect with something that has been lost in modern society: sensing the world through physical sensation rather than digital devices.

Clairvoyance is your ability to sense and understand things beyond what your five senses can detect.

https://www.pexels.com/photo/healthy-man-people-woman-6943955/

While most people don't inherently have this sixth sense, anyone can develop it with practice and dedication. This chapter will help you understand the Clairvoyant inside you by igniting your ability to see things beyond what your natural senses can detect.

What Are the Clair Senses?

The Clair senses are a set of supernormal abilities mentioned in multiple cultures and societies since time immemorial. Generally speaking, these involve the ability to see, hear, smell, or feel things that would normally be undetectable by human senses alone. They give us access to information about spirits, energy, and auras around us. Some claim that these senses let people see ghosts or spirits and communicate with them.

These senses were first brought to light by Rudolf Steiner in the early 20th century as part of his philosophical anthroposophy movement, which combined aspects of various other schools of thought, including Christianity, Hinduism, and Buddhism.

Many people today regard Clairvoyance (seeing), Clairsentience (feeling), Clairaudience (hearing), and Claircognizance (knowing) as esoteric or occult concepts. Whichever way you look at it, some people can perceive things more clearly than others. For most of us, this remains a mystery to gain knowledge on, but for some, it's a gift they were born with.

The Clair senses are psychic abilities you can develop with practice and patience. These include Clairvoyance and Clairaudience. People who develop these senses are known as Clairs. Although some people have stronger abilities than others, anyone can learn to strengthen their abilities through consistent practice. People with acute Clairvoyant skills tend to be more sensitive, perceptive, and more in tune with spiritual things around them.

Clairvoyance and Clairaudience are two types of psychic abilities. Both involve tapping into your sixth sense to know things without having to experience them firsthand. Clairvoyance is the ability to know what's going on in someone's life by visualizing it, while Clairaudience is the ability to hear what someone is thinking without them saying a word. If you want to develop these abilities, you can do so by clearing your mind and tuning out distractions so you can focus more clearly. Practicing gratitude to open yourself up to better things in your life will also be a great tool in your spiritual arsenal.

Clairvoyance (Seeing)

Since the dawn of time, humans have been fascinated by the idea of seeing beyond the visible, tangible world. From Merlin and his apprentice in "The Sword in the Stone" to Harry Potter and his schoolmates at Hogwarts, fictional characters who possess special abilities beyond what most people can see have captured our imagination. Now, as it turns out, these fictional stories are based on reality! You may be right if you've ever felt there was more to this world than what meets the eye. The concept of Clairvoyance originates from the French *Clair* (clear) and *voyance* (vision).

Thanks to Clairvoyance, you can intuitively understand what is going on in another person's life, either in the present or the future. It gives insight into other people's feelings, thoughts, and intentions, all with little information on their part. For example, if your best friend is feeling down but hasn't told you why, you might see it through Clairvoyance. Clairvoyant abilities typically involve clear visual images and feelings. You may see a vivid image of what's troubling your friend or feel like you're actually there. You may also see images of what hasn't happened yet but is likely to. Of course, the level of clarity varies from person to person. Some people experience their images as clearly as if they were watching a movie.

In contrast, others witness them as if they were watching them through a foggy window. As a Clairvoyant, you also can perceive things beyond the normal range of human perception. It can be defined as the ability to perceive information that cannot be obtained through the five ordinary senses. This includes seeing things that are not physically present and perceiving events in the past or future - independently and with other sensory information.

Signs That You Are Clairvoyant

Now that we've defined Clairvoyance, it's time to see if you have this special ability. Clairvoyant people often have an "open mind" and are aware of their surroundings. They tend to be keen observers and can pick up on details, often unconsciously. Clairvoyant people often have a higher-than-average IQ and can see things from a distance or in a non-sensory way. They may also be more creative and intuitive. They also excel at organizing things, especially when visualizing a situation to plan ahead. They also tend to be good at reading people and understanding what they want from them. Lastly, they have strong intuition, which can help them comprehend things better than others.

There are many ways to tell if you might have a gift of Clairvoyance. You might:

- Have dreams or visions that have come true
- Feel the presence of spirits
- See visions in your mind or on paper
- Learn things by intuition or feel other people's feelings
- Sense voices or images in your head.

In addition, you should consider your past experiences and how you were able to look into the future or know about something before it happened.

Developing Clairvoyant Abilities

You've probably heard about Clairvoyant abilities before, such as being "gifted" or "born with it." While there's no way to know whether you were born with Clairvoyant abilities, everyone can develop them. These include seeing things happening right now or in the future, and seeing what someone else is thinking or feeling. Some people have a natural ability for Clairvoyance and can see things almost immediately, whereas others take longer to develop them.

Here are a few useful tips for developing Clairvoyant abilities:

- Mind your surroundings. The more you pay attention to what is happening around you, the more likely you'll see things others miss.
- Think about what you want to see and visualize it clearly in your mind. This helps merge your Clairvoyance with your conscious thoughts and create a clearer vision of what is happening around you.
- Train yourself not to be afraid of what might be revealed; instead, embrace it as a gift from above.
- Incorporate meditation and relaxation techniques into your daily routine.
- Look for signs in your surroundings that suggest something is about to happen. Pay attention to things like unusual behavior in children or house pets or changes in the weather.
- Register for a reputable online course that will help you develop Clairvoyant abilities.
- Dream journaling is a superb way to bring your thoughts and feelings to the surface so you can explore them in greater depth. While you write, focus on whatever thoughts and feelings are on your mind.
- Researching Clairvoyance and other psychic abilities can help you better understand your own skills and learn how to hone them.
- Solicit an expert or Clairvoyant to see if they can help you develop your abilities.

In short, Clairvoyance is the ability to see through the mind's eye. The first step to accessing your mind's eye is to learn how to relax. Deep breathing and progressive muscle relaxation are two effective ways to alleviate stress and increase concentration. You can also use meditation techniques to open your mind's eyes. Sitting quietly, closing your eyes, and focusing on your breathing is the simplest yet most effective technique for opening your mind's eye. Other techniques you can use include visualizing yourself in a place you love to open up your heart or picturing yourself doing something you want to do to bolster your creative mind. Whatever works best for you - the goal is to practice opening your mind's eye so you can see what is happening around you.

Clairaudience (Hearing)

A person with clairaudience has the capacity to hear with exceptional clarity beyond the range of normal human hearing. This skill slightly differs from Clairvoyance, which is the ability to see beyond normal human sight. A person with this ability can hear subtle energies in the form of sounds that are inaudible to most people. Some call this ability "spiritual hearing," as they can hear spirits communicating with them through auditory tones. It's also closely related to Clairvoyance. Some people have the natural ability to hear and see things that other people cannot. Some may not even know about their hidden abilities until an unfortunate event triggers them. That said, there is no need to be afraid because these special powers can help you in many ways, whether at home, during a job interview, or even during a test at school. Let us take a closer look at Clairaudience and how it can help you in your everyday life.

Clairaudience is the ability to intuitively understand what is said and is happening around you, either in the present or the future. Like Clairvoyance, Clairaudience can sometimes be symbolic, like hearing an alarm clock ringing, but there's no alarm clock in the room. It can also be used to hear distant sounds, such as a bird singing in a tree or a train passing - or receive information about another person. You could also describe it as hearing something without anyone speaking. For example, if your friend is upset and doesn't tell you why you might tap into Clairaudience to know what's troubling them. Like Clairvoyance, Clairaudience can be visual or auditory. If you're upset and want to know what others think about you, Clairaudience can help with that, too. As useful as this ability is, external factors such as loud noises can be a disturbance, which can prevent you from perceiving any deeper sound.

Signs That You Are Clairaudient

If you possess Clairaudient abilities, you may be able to hear energy without any physical sound. It's an extrasensory perception that allows people to hear inner voices, sounds, and images. Clairaudience can manifest in many ways - from hearing your name called in public to catching the sounds of birds chirping or wind blowing. Although it isn't always clear whether the sounds are real or imagined, some people with Clairaudience feel a strong connection between their minds and the world around them. Clairaudients may also feel compelled to move objects with their mind and talk to themselves out loud. They may also suffer from sleep paralysis and experience vivid dreams. Some people with Clairaudience may have a family history of hearing voices or have experienced auditory hallucinations as a child. Some people describe it as a feeling of pressure in their ears that goes away after taking a deep breath. Others say they can hear colors or even taste them. Still, others report being able to hear things that are way out of their line of sight.

There are many ways to tell if you might have a gift of Clairaudience. You might:

- Be able to sense the emotions, health state, and other conditions of a person far from you
- Be able to communicate with someone who isn't physically present
- Retrieve lost objects or people
- Hear colors when perceiving the aura of other people. One way to describe this ability is "hearing from within." It may be part of the gift of empathy, otherwise known as empathic intuition.
- See the image of what's making someone angry or upset, or hearing them speaking to you although they never said a word
- See and hear something happening in another location or hear someone's thoughts or feelings.

Developing Clairaudient Abilities

Clairaudient abilities entail hearing sounds that others cannot hear. This can include all kinds of noises, from an electrical appliance's hum to an upset baby's cry. Some people may be born with this ability, but it can also be developed through training. Training for Clairaudience often involves listening to recorded sounds and identifying the source of each one. Learning to recognize and distinguish different sounds is essential to developing Clairaudience skills. Once you've learned how to recognize different noises, you can begin to hone your abilities, so you can reliably distinguish them.

There are many ways to develop Clairaudient abilities. Some people elect to use earplugs, while others wear headphones. Others wear special headbands or contact lenses to help tune out distracting noises. Whatever method you choose, practice regularly to build your skills and confidence.

Here are a few useful tips for developing Clairaudient abilities:

- Stay calm. This can help you quieten your thoughts so you can tune into the subtle energies or sounds around you.
- Be patient. Developing Clairaudience takes time and lots of patience to strengthen your ability.
- Practicing is the only way to develop your Clairaudience ability.
- Talk to yourself. This might sound strange, but it works. Doing so clears your mind of other thoughts and emotions so you can make room for new ones. This helps you tap into your intuition.
- You're more likely to tap into your intuition by focusing on one thing at a time and tuning out other distractions.

Meditation is great for quieting your mind and helping you focus. When you meditate, you clear your mind of other thoughts and emotions to pick up subtle energies and sounds around you. Try meditating on the sound of plants or even your own chakras.

- Try to record different sounds that you hear. This can help you identify the different sounds and frequencies.
- Identifying emotions can help you recognize the different emotions that you hear.
- Consulting various resources on developing Clairaudience can help you learn more about the ability.
- Working with a Clairaudient healer or Clairaudient reader can help you in your journey to develop Clairaudience.
- Since both are closely related, you can use Clairvoyance as a way to strengthen your Clairaudience ability.

How to Develop Your Clair Skills?

With consistent practice, you can improve your ability to access images and sounds that are beyond your senses. To improve your

Clairvoyance and Clairaudience, start by getting into a state of meditation:

1. Calm your body and mind so you can focus on receiving information. You can do this by sitting in a quiet and dark room or by walking outside and taking slow, deep breaths while tuning everything else out.
2. Remain calm. You might find that you're more relaxed when you do these exercises if you find a quiet spot where you can sit and relax without being distracted by noise or other people.
3. Next, focus your attention on what is happening around you. Close your eyes, take a deep breath, and tell yourself that you're about to receive information and images about specific people or things.
4. Open your eyes and focus on one person or object you want to receive information about. If it's a person, you can try tuning into their emotions and thoughts or focusing your attention on a specific object they're holding.
5. After you've received an image or a piece of information, write it down or speak it out loud so that you don't forget it. Try to meditate for at least 10 minutes every day, and make it a habit to try and receive information about people and things around you.

Remember that everyone has these abilities. Naturally, it's normal to feel a little anxious at first when attempting to access your Clairvoyant or Clairaudient abilities. These skills are part of your identity and can be developed with practice. This can be done by dedicating time to daily meditation and focusing on receiving information. You can also try to visualize the images and words you're receiving as you meditate. Once you've become more comfortable with these abilities, it should become easier to sharpen them.

5 Ways the Clairs Can Help You

Clairvoyance and Clairaudience are just two examples of what are known as secondary senses. These senses can be developed with practice and patience. There's no magic or witchcraft involved here - anyone willing to invest time in developing them can do so successfully.

1. **Identifying different energies**: With the help of the Clairs, you can easily identify different energies around you. This can enable you to stay away from harmful energies.
2. **Improve your relationships:** The Clairs can help you better understand your partner, friends, and relatives. It can help you bring out the best in your relationships.
3. **Healing:** The Clairs can also help you in healing. Whether you're a trained healer or an enthusiast, you can use your Clairaudience to heal yourself or the people around you.
4. **In your job:** The Clairs can help you identify subtle sounds and sense things around your workplace. You'll be able to perform better at work and connect with others as a result.
5. **Studying:** The Clairs can help you study better. You can focus better on your lessons, boost your focus, and be more receptive to new knowledge from professors and peers.

A Word of Caution

Psychic powers are the ability to sense, see and communicate with other realms or dimensions. However, these powers can result from several factors, including genetics, trauma, stress, and even physical illness. Psychics and their clients often report feeling uncomfortable, confused, and anxious after a session. This could be because they may not understand what is happening during their session or because they're unsure about the legitimacy of the psychic's abilities. Moreover, some psychics may use their abilities to exploit vulnerable people; using psychic powers is not always positive. It's important to remember that only you know what your body is capable of doing and what you can handle.

Note: You may be hearing voices or seeing things not only due to the Clairs but also *mental illnesses*. Consult a licensed professional if you feel confused, insecure, or anxious about your mental health. All Clair senses, including telepathy, are subject to this disclaimer.

A lot can be said about developing your Clairvoyance and Clairaudience abilities. Ultimately, Clairvoyance doesn't come easy to most people. It takes patience, perseverance and practice to develop and use this special skill in your everyday life. The ability to see beyond what is normally perceived opens up a whole new world of possibilities.

It can allow you to see what others cannot hear and understand what others cannot understand. It's an amazing gift to work with, whether you can see into the future or not.

Chapter 3: The Clairs II. Psychic Knowing and Feeling

Did you know that your mind is a virtual warehouse of untapped potential? You can unlock clairvoyant abilities known as Claircognizance and Clairsentience using hidden parts of your mind. These Clairs are another set of intuitive senses that describe specific manifestations of intuition, specifically knowing and feeling.

You can unlock clairvoyant abilities known as Claircognizance and Clairsentience using hidden parts of your mind.

https://www.pexels.com/photo/city-landscape-fashion-man-6669855/

If you're reading this, it's probably because you've experienced some kind of odd premonition or sensed something with your sixth sense. Chances are you're not alone. These experiences are common for people who have discovered their hidden psychic abilities or "Clairs." In this chapter, we'll further explore the world of the Clairs and how they can help boost your intuition and inner knowing.

What Makes Us Want to Know and Feel?

We live in a time of rekindled interest in the paranormal, spirituality, and other "taboo" topics that have typically been ignored or dismissed as nonsense. This is especially true for phenomena that most people find inherently uninteresting or unbelievable. Few things fall under this category more than the sixth sense, which is the ability to perceive the world beyond our natural senses. However, with almost every corner of the internet exploding with videos about aliens, ghosts, or spirits, it's no wonder that interest in these Clair senses has skyrocketed as of late. Practitioners claim that they can read energy and pick up on the thoughts and emotions of others - whether human or non-human entities.

Today, people are seeking new ways to unplug and find peace. We're witnessing the rise of meditation apps, yoga studios, and mindfulness practices. In this new age of spirituality, we also see increasing interest in knowing what truly matters. This is because people want more than just a guided meditation, where a stranger tells them what to think about for 20 minutes. They want something that's tailor-made for their needs and interests. That's why people are looking for Clair techniques and exercises that go beyond reading books, listening to lectures, or watching videos on the topic. With the help of the Clairs, you can expand your mind's horizons and reach new levels of perception that you didn't know were possible.

Claircognizance (Knowing)

Chances are you've been curious about your Claircognizant abilities. If you have an interest in the paranormal and all things mysterious, wonderful, and strange, then Claircognizance is the perfect ability for you. The term "Claircognizance" means having a heightened intuition combined with knowledge from an outside source. This may sound like something from Harry Potter or even The Twilight Zone - after all, most of us don't know much about Clairvoyance or Clairsentience. However, they both describe what many people might simply refer to as that "sixth sense."

Claircognizance is a mode of consciousness best described as clear or inner knowing. It's something we all have inside us - you just have to know how to access it. This psychic ability is often referred to as a "hunch," an "intuitive hit," or a "gut feeling." While some people rely on Clairvoyance to receive information, Claircognizant people rely on their ability to "know" information. Claircognizance occurs when you receive a strong insight or impression about something. For example, if you're trying to decide between two jobs or two college classes, and you just know that you need to take one over the other, that is Claircognizance at work.

Signs That You Are Claircognizant

Being Claircognizant means having "mindsight," in other words, the ability to see in your mind what other people are seeing and feeling. Claircognizant people are aware of their surroundings. They notice details, such as whether someone looks uncomfortable or where the nearest restroom is located. They also know when something feels unusual and can name the cause. If you are Claircognizant, you know what's going on around you. You're present and aware and can understand what other people don't see. This means that your senses are working to their best and that you're processing everything you experience healthily. If you feel your senses aren't working at optimal capacity, your diet is one of the first things to (re)consider. In fact, eating a carbohydrate-rich diet can lead to a decrease in blood glucose levels, which can make it harder for your brain to function properly. You also need to ensure you're getting enough sleep so that your body can recover and re-energize itself for the next day.

As established, Claircognizance is an intuition, so the signs will vary from person to person. The best way to figure out if you have this psychic ability is to pay attention to your feelings, dreams, and overall gut instinct.

There are many ways to tell if you might have a gift of Claircognizance. Ask yourself:

- Do you have a constant gut instinct?
- Are you always feeling like something is right or wrong?

- Do you just "know" that something will happen?
- Do you often have strong emotional reactions to certain situations?

If you find that you constantly rely on your gut or instinct, it could be your Claircognizance at work. While many Clairvoyants experience prophetic dreams, Claircognizants often receive different types of messages in their sleep. Suppose you often dream about future events or different people, places, and situations with which you have no connection. In that case, this could be your Claircognizance manifesting itself. Have you ever been in a situation where you knew exactly what to do, even if you had never been in that situation before? Did it feel like you knew the outcome before you even took action? If yes, this could be your Claircognizance kicking in.

Developing Claircognizance Abilities

You must first unblock your energy to develop Claircognizance and become more in tune with your inner voice. Many people subconsciously block their Clairvoyance due to past experiences or emotions. However, it's crucial to unblock your energy so your abilities can blossom fully. Otherwise, your psychic gifts will be inhibited. Now that you know what Claircognizance is and understand its signs, it's time to unblock your energy and allow your Claircognizance to thrive.

Here are some helpful tips for unblocking your Claircognizance:

- **Exercise:** Physical exercise releases endorphins and gets your blood flowing. By engaging in physical activity regularly, you'll increase your serotonin levels, which are key in unblocking your energy.
- **Meditate:** Meditation grounds you and gets in touch with your innermost thoughts and emotions. It helps you become mindful of how you're feeling and what you're thinking.
- **Dream journaling**: Journaling is an effective way to get in touch with your emotions. By writing down your thoughts and feelings, you can better understand yourself.
- **Talking to a therapist:** Seeing a therapist is a great way to work through past experiences that are negatively affecting you. This can be helpful for gaining clarity about the blockages in your life and how to overcome them and move forward.

Clairsentience (Feeling)

If you've ever experienced sudden intuition about someone or something, you're likely a Clairsentient soul - a soul who can sense and intuit information through their sixth sense. They can sense things that most people cannot detect with their regular senses. In fact, they know things mostly based on intuition rather than direct observation. Since this is such an uncommon ability, it's helpful to understand what makes someone a Clairsentient individual. Let's take a closer look at how Clairsentience works, who can possess it, and why some people may not even know they have the ability until it's triggered.

Clairsentience is the ability to sense and feel the emotions of people, animals, plants, and even inanimate objects. Clairsentient individuals are referred to as "sensitive" or "highly sensitive" people because they're more likely to be aware of subtler stimuli than most. Since the sensitivity of Clairsentients is so unique, it's also important to understand what makes them different from other people. Like many things about these individuals, their heightened intuition can be attributed to their inherent nature and experiences.

How Does Clairsentience Work?

Aside from being an extrasensory perception, Clairsentience is an ability to perceive information about the outside world without using the five traditional senses. Just like there are different types of sensory receptors in our eyes, ears, nose, etc., there are also different receptors inside our bodies. These receptors send and receive information from the environment and our surroundings. The theory is that Clairsentients have a heightened sensitivity to these receptors. This allows them to perceive and feel subtle energies others cannot perceive or notice. The brain then interprets these signals as feelings or emotions. Although it's not certain how Clairsentience works, many believe that people with these heightened abilities have a lower threshold for stimulation than average.

Signs That You Are a Clairsentient

Clairsentients can experience the world in a radically different way. Typically, they can describe the emotions of others, smell or taste negative vibes, and even receive information from inanimate objects like maps or books that others have handled. The human energy field is made up of various kinds of subtle energy. Clairsentience is the ability to feel energy or "vibes" from a person, place, or object. People with Clairsentience abilities can feel vibrations in the air and detect the emotions, thoughts, and intent of the people around them. Moreover, some Clairsentient people can hear voices and sounds from other dimensions. They can also sense when a loved one is nearby and know what they're feeling simply by sensing the emotion in their surroundings.

There are many ways to tell if you might have the gift of Clairsentience, including:

- You are intuitive
- You have a deep connection with nature and animals
- You feel emotions such as sadness or anger more intensely than others
- You feel anxious when in a highly stimulating environment
- You prefer quiet, undistracted environments
- You are empathetic toward others
- You are highly creative and artistic
- You have a strong imagination
- You are sensitive to light, sound, smells, and taste
- You are sensitive to touch
- You have low blood pressure or a strong pulse
- You feel a constant need to cleanse yourself and your surroundings

Developing Clairsentience Abilities

You can develop Clairsentience by performing mindfulness exercises, meditation, or aromatherapy to raise your chakra levels. You can also work with crystals and gemstones to enhance your psychic abilities. Some Clairaudient people may even use tarot cards to gain insight into a particular situation. Clairsentience can be developed in several ways, including practicing and learning how to use these abilities. This may include seeking out other people with the same abilities as you, reading books and articles about Clairsentient abilities, and developing the skills necessary to use them. There are no real rules on how much practice is needed, as it depends on each individual's needs. Like any new skill, however, the more you do it, the better you'll get at it. So, be patient, and keep practicing.

Here are some helpful tips on how to unblock your Clairaudience:

- Pray or meditate to open your mind and sense all the energies around you.
- Picture yourself surrounded by white light and visualize any negative vibes being cleansed away.
- Get in touch with your feelings and be mindful of how you feel.
- Be creative. Visual and creative activities stimulate the right side of the brain, which is associated with clairaudience.
- Be empathetic. Shift your focus from yourself and toward others.
- Be aware of your surroundings. Take note of any odd feelings or vibes you might be getting from a certain place.
- Stay positive and surround yourself with positive folks. Because negativity can shut down your psychic abilities, avoid hanging out with people who always complain and drain your energy.
- Keep an open mind. Try not to dismiss your intuitions or gut feelings as silly or ridiculous, as things that don't make sense can often become clairvoyant visions.
- Be patient. Developing these abilities takes time, so don't get frustrated if you don't see immediate results.

If you think you can sense and feel emotions, but you aren't sure, start paying more attention to your surroundings and the people around you. If you're in a crowded environment, try to focus on just their energies and emotions. Pick one person and imagine what they might be feeling. From there, move on to the next person. As you do this, visualize the emotions as colors. This will help you lock in on what you're feeling with better accuracy. Another way you can practice this skill is by focusing on your own feelings. What emotions do you feel if you're in a calm and happy place? Do you feel happy or excited? By practicing this on yourself, you can train yourself to feel the emotions of others around you.

More Possible Clair Senses That You Might Have

A Clairvoyant person is often depicted as an old mystic with a snowy beard and long, unkempt hair. However, this image doesn't reflect the truth about Clairvoyants. There are many Clair abilities any regular person can have. It's like a light that can be switched on in your third eye or sixth sense. Let's find out exactly what some of the other Clair abilities are and if you can recognize them in yourself.

Clairalience

Clairalience is the ability to feel heightened awareness that can be described as "being in the moment." It occurs when you can perceive and respond to your surroundings with greater, more accurate perception. This can result from various factors, including ambient noise levels, distractions, overstimulation, or any combination of these. Clairalience is an umbrella term to describe any enhanced awareness that can lead to positive outcomes. It can be triggered by the environment we live in or by our interactions with other people. For some, it can even be triggered by certain emotions or situations. It's important to note that there is no one-size-fits-all definition for Clairalience since everyone will experience it in different ways. The key is to be aware when you're experiencing heightened perception and take advantage of whatever opportunities arise from this state.

Clairalience commonly describes sensations of well-being or euphoria. In fact, it's distinct from and often confused with euphoria. Euphoria is an emotional state characterized by feelings of happiness and excitement. Because it's an emotional experience, it can be difficult to distinguish between euphoria and Clairalience. However, the difference is that, while euphoria is short-lived, Clairalience can feel like a more sustained high. Many things, including exercise, meditation, and walks in nature, can induce Clairalience. While it's often associated with positive emotions, it can also be experienced in response to negative experiences, such as trauma or stress.

In addition, Clairalience doesn't necessarily have to be experienced consciously. For example, a dog who has just played fetch might be experiencing Clairalience without knowing it. A common misconception about Clairalience is that it always means you feel happy or blissful.

While feelings of happiness often accompany feelings of well-being, they can also be associated with other internal states, like anxiety and sadness.

How to Practice Clairalience

Be present *in the moment*, fully engaged in what you're doing, and observe your surroundings. The more aware you are of your surroundings and the emotions of those around you, the better you will understand their feelings and empathize with them.

Pay attention to the sensations you feel in your body and your surroundings. For example, if someone is upset in the office, notice how their body feels as they walk by you.

- Are they tensed or shaky?
- How do their shoulders look?
- Do they look tired or stressed?
- Are there any physical signs that might reveal whether or not their stress level is high?

Next, try to empathize with others' emotions by imagining how they feel when they are experiencing different situations. This can help you put yourself in their shoes and better understand why they might feel the way they do.

Clairtangency

Clairtangency is the ability to sense or "feel" the presence of another person, which can be perceived through various senses, such as vibrations or smells. Clairtangency is often described as an "open line" with someone's spirit or soul. It can lead to a deep connection between two people, whether a friendship or a romantic relationship. This sense is often described as a feeling of comfort, serenity, and safety near another person. It can be felt both physically and mentally. The physical sensation of being close to another person may include warmth, tingling sensations, or even rumbling sounds if they touch the skin. Clairtangency is sometimes called "feeling energy" because it is not always easy to put into words.

Many people with this ability claim to "feel" the flow of time in their own bodies. While anyone can experience it, some describe it as being able to feel time flowing through their hands or feet. It's a form of Clairvoyance where a person can sense the texture of an object and understand its origins, such as when someone has handled the object and left their energy behind. This phenomenon usually occurs when a person is under extreme emotional stress. Because there are no concrete scientific explanations for how this ability works, it has been compared to other unexplained phenomena, such as ESP and other psychic abilities.

How to Practice Clairtangency

You can decode the messages being sent by people and objects around you by paying attention to your surroundings and picking up on subtle energy signals.

Tuning into your own energy body is the next step. This is where you'll find your chakras and other energetic centers. It is possible to detect subtle changes in your energy by tuning into these areas of your body. You might experience these changes when you feel anxious, tired, or disrupted by the energy field around you.

Once you've mastered this area, practice on a meaningful object in your life; with a little time, you will begin to see a shift in the surrounding energy field when holding this object. You can then apply your new awareness to unfamiliar objects from the past. If you have Clairtangency, they will speak to you.

Clairgustance

Clairgustance is the ability to taste and smell a flavor that isn't present in the environment. This can be related to the past, present, or future. It combines your sense of smell and the ability to perceive scents from other people. You can experience it if you have ever smelled someone else's perfume or cologne or if you have been close enough to someone else to smell their body odor or sweat. Clairgustance is a form of extrasensory perception (ESP). It can be experienced as a tingling sensation in the back of the throat or an overwhelming sense that something amazing is nearby. Clairgustance may also point to something else, such as an impending disaster. For example, if you were standing near a spot and suddenly smelled smoke, indicating a potential fire, you would have Clairgustance. That said, it's not always easy to tell what is going on when you encounter this kind of feeling. It can be a little scary if you don't know how to interpret it.

Clairgustance is not just about smelling something in someone else's presence, like their perfume - it also includes detecting smells from far away. In addition, if you can detect the smells of food cooking at home on a very early morning before anyone has had breakfast, you may have Clairgustance. This heightened Clair can be due to genetics and lifestyle choices, such as consuming certain foods or beverages, past-life memories, and stress levels and hormones.

How to Practice Clairgustance

There is much more to tasting and smelling than many people realize. By training yourself to discern flavors, you're training your mind to become more discerning in all other areas of your life. Sharpening your sense of smell can also allow you to pick up on subtle emotions, which can be helpful for those who work with the dead or tend to be psychically sensitive.

So, where do you start? First, relax your mind and body, then take a deep breath and try to focus on your sense of smell. What do you smell? Start by noticing the strongest scents in the air, and then work your way down your nose to the tip of your tongue. Focus on whether you get a negative or positive feeling associated with the smell.

There are a few general rules you should follow when practicing taste and smell:

- Try not to eat or drink anything while trying to train your senses.
- Start a scent journal to track your experiences with different scents over time.
- Practice in a clean environment, as concentrating on several smells can confuse your senses.

Lastly, remember that it takes time to get used to being able to detect these things, typically anywhere between a few hours and a few days.

The ability to know and feel subtle energies is a unique gift that not everyone inherently possesses. Fortunately, this chapter and the previous one will have given you a better understanding of these special abilities and how to develop them. When they're present, they can be an incredibly enriching and rewarding experience for both the individual and those around them. While it can sometimes be difficult to identify these special individuals, once you know what to look for, it's easy to spot them in any crowd. If you feel what we've discussed resonates with you, don't hesitate to explore these special abilities and discover what they can teach you about yourself and your purpose.

Chapter 4: Psychic Protection and Shielding

Being a psychic or medium often means engaging in an extended exercise in vulnerability while also working hard to protect yourself from said vulnerability. The capacity for such openness and a willingness to connect with others is a unique gift, but it must be nurtured and protected. Using your psychic capabilities means working with your energies more than you normally would, so it's important to *proceed with caution.* If you're not careful, you may end up soaking up everyone's thoughts and negative vibes, which will inevitably impact your life in unpleasant ways. The key to being a successful medium is learning to balance your own needs as an individual with the needs of others you'll be helping. This dedicated chapter will guide you and provide some useful pointers to help you protect yourself from unwanted influences.

If you're not careful, you may end up soaking up everyone's thoughts and negative vibes.
https://www.pexels.com/photo/woman-in-white-shirt-holding-orange-and-white-lollipop-6943953/

Barring "Invasions"

Looking at matters through a metaphysical lens, the world is made up of energies - it's the way things come into being and how everyone communicates. As biological creatures, clueing into this pool of energy is essential to how we evolve and connect with other beings in the world. The downside of this is that our processes are malleable, easily influenced, and can cause us to go down a million divergent paths. It's really a "choose your own adventure" sort of game, which is why one must be careful as a psychic.

At the same time, no one can invade your energy source unless you let them, so rest assured that you have some control over the matter. Each individual is ultimately the gatekeeper of their energy field, so you won't easily get roped into anything if you don't want to. Luckily, no alien being will come rushing into your body, taking over without your consent. Part of the work you will need to master is preventing your open nature from becoming too open and figuring out the best pace for you. However, all of that work begins with a clear sense of your own powers and the fact that you are in control, not the other way around. Without a clear understanding of these power dynamics, you won't be able to master these techniques and may run the risk of letting the universe wreak more havoc on your life than you bargained for. Harmful spirits or entities with bad intentions may feel free to use you as their vessel, and your energies will deplete quickly.

For that reason, getting the hang of psychic protection and shielding is an absolute must-have skill for any psychic to possess, whether or not they're new to the practice. Fortunately, a plethora of cleansing, protection, shielding, and banishing rituals exist, not only for yourself but for the people you're trying to help. There's also a multitude of smudging rituals, prayers, and chants you can fill the home with if your main interest is to protect a physical space like the home. Some of these techniques have a long history and are so popular that you may have noticed smudge sticks, crystals, and the like being sold on the market, sometimes for a hefty price tag. In reality, some of these practices are simpler than you'd think.

Smudge Sticks

Let's begin with one of the simpler techniques to guarantee you and your space protection: smudge sticks. These are bunches of herbs bound together by twine. Certain herbs are selected for their specific properties, with some of the most popular being rosemary, white sage, or Yerba Santa. Depending on your specific needs at any given moment, you can combine different herbs or simply stick to one bunch of the same. Then, when you're ready, you burn the herbs and wave the smoke in the direction of the person or space you'd like to offer the protection. The act of burning the smudge stick is known as smudging, hence the name.

Various cultures and peoples have practiced this ancient ritual in many places. Native Americans, in particular, used smudge sticks to clear out low vibrations or any energies that felt stuck in a particular place. They believed that the act of smudging helped create positive energy and allowed people to lift their spirits. If you're looking to protect yourself, you can point the smoke toward your own body and then wave the burning stick in different directions throughout the home to ensure that your living space is similarly full of positive energy and is well protected from any negative vibes.

Banishment Rituals

This is a more involved form of shielding yourself from being too open and safeguarding your psychic abilities. Banishment rituals are complicated but important to master and perform from time to time, depending on the context. To perform this, you will need the following:

- **An altar:** In the center of your ritual space, regardless of where you choose to set it up, is your altar, as well as the instruments representing the four classical elements. Classical elements are what we know as earth, water, air, and fire. Modern occultists have also introduced aether, also known as the fifth element of quintessence. This material fills the area of the universe just beyond the terrestrial sphere. This element serves to explain different kinds of natural phenomena, such as the traveling of light and gravity, whose nature isn't necessarily represented within the other four elements.

The next two elements are optional and ultimately boil down to your own beliefs:

- Those practicing magic typically wore ceremonial robes or ritual garb.
- A ritual sword or athame. This is used to gesture toward different points of the cross and to help draw pentagrams if you so choose.

First and foremost, create the astral cross in your body by pointing to the areas that correspond with the understanding of the Tree of Life, repairing the words forehead, feet, right shoulder, left shoulder, and heart, respectively. Extra points if you can say these words in Hebrew to follow the Kabbalah tradition.

Next, formulate the pentagrams, beginning in the East, saying the names of the negative energies you need to banish. You can visualize these in blue light or light a candle as you work and focus on the burning flame. This part of the ritual is meant to invoke the elements as you simultaneously banish whatever is causing you trouble. The four pentagrams are connected by a circle, which is also drawn in the air. You would typically start from the North point to the East point.

The third step can be adjusted according to what you're looking for and your own set of beliefs. However, they tend to follow the Kabbalah version by invoking the archangels, a part of the ceremony that entails the psychic standing in front of the cross at the altar and declaring that the archangels Raphael, Gabriel, Michael, and Uriel are all present, visualizing them as the four cardinal points.

Finally, this is repeated another time to ensure that the spirits are banished and that your aura and home are cleansed accordingly.

Safeguarding Packets and Tools

We discussed smudge sticks earlier, which are a simple yet essential tool in any psychic's arsenal. Another bundle that is good to keep on hand is a patch of palo santo and selenite. Together, the herb and the powerful crystal will help keep you safe - the palo santo is great for clearing away any lingering negativity in your home, while selenite can help prevent bad vibes from making their way in. It is advisable to keep this little bundle near your front door as an effective safety precaution.

Do you need extra protection when you're outside the home? Carry around some crystals to help protect you from any unwanted forces and their influences. One protective stone that can help you safeguard your aura and prevent you from being too open is black tourmaline. They're shiny, rough, and jagged. Still, these modest-looking specimens are excellent for protection and are easy to carry in your back pocket. You can also keep them at your office desk or at your home library if these are spaces you feel may be *porous* and tend to attract bad energy. Keeping these crystals around will help you feel secure and strong.

Sachets are another excellent way to keep you protected. These little packets not only smell lovely, but they help to safeguard you against unwanted forces. They're generally made up of basil, rosemary, star anise, juniper berries, and other herbs and essential oils like lavender rose or orange. You can look up different mixes and choose the relevant herbs according to your needs. Sachets are excellent for your home, office, and even your car. If you carry a bag with you everywhere you go, you can also put a little sachet in there. All you have to do is create your blend and scoop them into a little pouch, hanging them wherever you like.

If you like to keep things simple, go with the classic solution of using salt to banish bad vibes and protect yourself from unwanted emotions or energies. Throw salt over your shoulder the old-fashioned way, or get into the habit of salting the corners of your room and the doorway to your home. Obviously, this often gets messy, so you can keep a small bowl of salt near the areas in question to help eliminate negative energy.

Aligning the Chakras

One excellent way of ensuring you're protecting yourself and your energy reserves as you pursue psychic work is to ensure that your chakras are aligned. You can engage in different exercises to help you with this. For one, the popular auric egg exercise is a good step toward meditation that allows you to breathe in and visualize warm light making its way to different chakra centers in your body.

For starters, sit down with your back straight while maintaining a relaxed position. Then, visualize yourself within an oval-shaped field (like an egg, hence the name) that extends toward the center of your body and stretches three feet in every direction. Mentally trace the egg shape from the highest point you can imagine from your head, focusing on a pure white color-led light leading the way. While you can perform the exercise using different colors, white light is the most effective way to imagine a peaceful aura surrounding you, working to keep you safe from bad energies.

The next step involves anchoring this bright white light in the center of your body while taking deep breaths, feeling the beat of your heart, and allowing it to resonate throughout your body. These steadying breaths are key to helping you feel calm and at peace. Then, on one breath, imagine light entering your body and as you exhale, allow the light to expand and fill your head, then your arms, back, torso, and feet. You should be able to feel the light moving in every direction to ignite your chakras and allow you to feel comforted. Continue to breathe and visualize the light moving around you, thereby banishing anything that doesn't serve you while centering your body.

Meditate for at least five to ten minutes until your body feels calmer and more relaxed. Doing this daily ensures that you maintain your energy source, making it more difficult for other energies to enter without your consent. It's a way of "future-proofing" your mind and body so that you're not allowing different thoughts or vibes to enter as you use your psychic abilities. Meditating for a few minutes a week should help you meet your goals without trouble.

Cultivating Awareness

As mentioned, meditation is one way of cultivating an awareness of your body and thoughts. Being empathetic is a wonderful and essential trait any good psychic should have. However, it can also be taxing, especially if you're not taking the appropriate steps to protect yourself.

Daily affirmations are like incantations you can use to help you stay attuned to your body and needs. There isn't one that you need to follow in a textbook fashion - you can draft whichever version you like. For example, you can write or say to yourself something along the lines of: "My energy can rise to high levels and has the capacity to rid my home and other places of evil. A bright light follows me, and I can help the people I love and care for." You can incorporate this affirmation into any daily ritual you've devised for yourself - it can end a meditation session, a yoga workout, candle burning ritual, or you use a smudge stick throughout the home.

You can also write it down daily, first thing in the morning. While journaling may be an odd thing to mention in the context of psychic protection and shielding, it definitely has a place in your bid to become more aware of your "self" and the different energies coursing throughout your body and the universe. For example, you can start your day by noting which areas in your life seem to deplete your energy the most. Alternatively, pinpoint places that you'd like to make stronger and bring more focus to in your daily life. Once you have a list in hand, you can zero in on it and begin to whittle down the things that have been upsetting to you or the relationships you recognize need more work. Then, focus your powers on solving them one by one.

You can also get into the habit of writing down different things you've noticed throughout the day. Take notice of the things around you or the different places in your practice that may need to be refined. Commit yourself to one to two pages a day. This is a simple way of cleansing your aura and clearing your mind, making you a more powerful and steady psychic medium over time.

Practicing psychic work isn't a walk in the park. It requires constant practice and attunement to different areas in life you hope to focus on. While there are many elaborate rituals you can pursue or crystals you can buy, a lot of this work falls to you. It's imperative to recognize that you must listen to your inner self and maintain your energy levels accordingly. As a psychic, focusing on the past is actually not a great idea - working hard to make yourself stronger mentally and emotionally in the future is the best way to protect your unique gifts and hone them.

Chapter 5: Divination Tools for Psychics

Divination practices are often employed to predict future events by seeking guidance from the unknown. Each technique uses different tools to perform the reading. Interpreting these readings is also an essential part, which is where the psychics come in. Psychics have an enhanced sensory perception that allows them to use certain tools to perform divination. Throughout history, there have been many methods of divination. While some of these divination techniques have faded over time, many are still frequently used for psychic readings.

Divination practices are often employed to predict future events by seeking guidance from the unknown.

https://www.pexels.com/photo/healthy-wood-man-love-6944906/

Psychics have employed countless divination tools to make predictions and interpretations for centuries. Using these tools is not mandatory for a psychic, as they can do well without them. However, using divination tools for psychic readings only enhances the quality and accuracy of the readings. Today, the most commonly used divination tools include pendulums, tarot cards, astrology, scrying, dowsing, runes, i-ching coins, and many more. This chapter will dive deeply into the world of divination tools and equip you with all the knowledge you need regarding these tools.

Pendulums

Pendulum magic is one of the most popular divination techniques that provide insightful results. A pendulum is basically a crystal, rock, or metal hanging at the end of a chain. Traditionally, this technique is used to locate hidden water or other valuable materials. People also use it to seek answers and guidance regarding their problems. The principle of pendulum magic is based on energy manifestation. Essentially, everything in this world has unique energy or vibration - in this case, the crystal of the pendulum manifests its energy and draws upon the energy of the space to provide answers.

Today, pendulums are used in all kinds of rituals and psychic readings. A common method is to hover the pendulum over a paper with "yes" and "no" written. You're supposed to concentrate on the question you wish to answer and set your intention. The pendulum does the rest. Getting a pendulum board with multiple answers to your questions is also common practice. This will help you understand the reading better and assist with the interpretation.

Pendulums are pretty simple instruments, so they can be easily personalized if you want to create your own unique pendulum. You can select a crystal that has personal significance to you or is proven to help your task. Each crystal has a specific kind of energy and is therefore used for specific purposes.

Crystal Balls

The use of crystal balls is overwhelmingly popular among psychics, according to popular culture. In contrast, the technique of using a crystal ball to envision shapes and visions of the future is a meticulous and highly challenging process. Mastering this technique only comes with tremendous practice and patience, which only a few can achieve. The technique itself is called scrying, which helps the seeker gain insight into the future. It's the process of gazing into a reflective surface, in this case, a crystal ball, and using your intuition and psychic abilities to attract any messages from the universe in the form of shapes, visions, and images.

These images can then be interpreted with regard to the circumstances or background information to form a deeper understanding of the issue. While most are made of clear quartz, you can use any type of crystal for making a crystal ball. Generally, amethyst, calcite, and even obsidian crystals are used to design crystal balls for scrying and divination.

Crystals

Crystals hold a unique place in the world of psychics. They're used in many divination tools and even separately for divination purposes. As explained before, crystals have a unique energy signature that helps connect psychics to their inner wisdom and intuition. When using crystals, trusting one's gut feeling or sixth sense is the most crucial part. If you can't trust your intuition, no divination tool will be able to help you. In that regard, crystals assist with connecting with your intuition as they're able to build a bridge between the spiritual world and your own. Each type of crystal specializes in the clearance of a specific chakra. For instance, amazonite is said to enhance emotional intelligence, whereas amethyst helps clear the crown chakra.

Tarot Cards

Another well-known divination tool, tarot cards, is frequently used by psychics to receive guidance about past, present, and future scenarios. The deck of tarot cards consists of 78 cards, with 56 Minor Arcana and 22 Major Arcana. Each card is unique in its own way, featuring an illustration that can be interpreted in different ways. The position of the card also matters when interpreting the reading. For instance, if the illustration is upside down or upright, it will have a different meaning. Moreover, the sequence of the cards will also change the outcome of the reading.

To practice this technique, you simply need to lay out a few cards after setting the intention of the reading. Next, depending on the position of each card, you'll need to interpret them based on the seeker's background. You should preferably use a tarot card guide at first to understand what each illustration means and how to interpret the positions. After a while, you'll start to get the hang of it and make more accurate readings.

It is said that the Major Arcana are connected with the life lessons that must be completed throughout one's lifetime. On the other hand, the Minor Arcana cards are associated with the day-to-day experiences and ordeals one has to face. Each deck of tarot cards also contains 16 Court cards. These cards symbolize the personality traits of the seeker. Another category in the tarot deck includes the Suits, representing the four elements of nature.

Contrary to popular belief, tarot card readings are more concerned with intuition and guidance rather than fortune-telling. The knowledge gained from these readings helps strengthen one's intuition and sense of perception. Aside from being simple to understand and learn, tarot cards are great tools for psychic development. While this technique doesn't necessarily provide direct answers, you'll be free to interpret the readings as you see fit.

Ouija Board

Here's another divination technique whose popularity mainly owes to the entertainment industry. Almost everyone is familiar with the Ouija board and how it's used. However, unlike the popular idea that they're only used for contacting spirits, Ouija boards can be employed for various divination purposes. These boards are engraved with numbers 1 to 9 and all the alphabet. A "yes" and "no" are also available on the board for easy communication.

To practice this divination method, carefully put your fingers on top of the triangular piece of the Ouija board. Then, you need to concentrate on the question you need to be answered. The spirit or universal guides will move the planchette toward the answer it wants to give. While performing this practice, you must be cautious as it can open up a pathway for negative spirits and risk possession.

Dowsing Rods

Dowsing is another popular divination method traditionally used to detect hidden objects and water sources. This method is a little different compared to other typical divination methods, considering it isn't used to predict future circumstances but instead for seeking guidance and finding hidden information from universal guides. Today, psychics employ this method to identify when they come across a spirit. You'll likely encounter a spirit or guide present to help you during the practice. When you do, the dowsing rods you're holding will make a cross or X shape. When you observe this, ask your questions.

To practice this technique, hold the dowsing rods lightly from the ends. You'll witness the rods automatically moving upward or downward when you find what you're looking for, whether it's hidden minerals, precious ore, water, or a spirit. You must continually practice using the dowsing rods to familiarize yourself with the technique before you use them for a serious matter.

Oracle Cards

Oracle cards, often confused with tarot cards, can serve as a daily form of spiritual guidance. They're often combined with tarot cards to get a detailed reading but can also be used separately for a standard reading. These cards come with special messages and don't have a specific number of cards. You could get an oracle card deck of about 30 cards or maybe one with just 12 cards. Besides the illustrations and symbols on these cards, they're equipped with poetic statements that provide deep insight into one's life situation. Many oracle cards have Celtic themes, while others relate to astrology.

Considering the non-traditional nature of these cards, many practitioners don't get the hang of them. Therefore, don't be surprised if it takes a while to figure out the themes and concepts behind these cards. You may even feel frustrated at times, but don't give up. Usually, oracle cards are used to make one-card-a-day readings, but some psychics even make three-card readings for reflection.

Scrying Mirrors

Like crystal ball reading techniques, scrying mirrors predict future events using a reflective surface. The practitioner will get visions or images when gazing deeply into the reflective surface, which will be relevant to the questions asked. Usually, this method is carried out using a crystal ball or plain mirrors, but if you don't have access to these, you can always opt for a bowl of clear water. Scrying requires a reflective surface, so mirrors aren't a prerequisite for this method. Although this is a very effective method of divination, people seldom get close to mastering this art. It takes both time and practice to master the technique of scrying. The practitioner will have to be in complete sync with their intuition and spirituality. In the event of an inability to master this process, the practitioner will get hard to decipher results and thus face difficulty.

I-Ching Coins

The use of I-Ching coins is another traditional divination method, dating as far back as 2700 BC. This method manifests the yin and yang energy to find meaning and make predictions. In older versions of this divination tool, the coins used to be engraved with yin and yang symbols, but today, they've become vastly modified and contain many variations of engravings. Start by assigning each symbol to the two sides of a coin. Once you've done this, toss the coin and write down the results. Repeat these five more times, and you'll get a pattern of results or code that will translate as a hexagram number. Use a guidebook to interpret this number, and you'll get your results.

Runes

Runes are ancient symbols used to communicate between the Scandinavian people, which is where this method originates. In time, these runes became a means of divination and were printed on small stones or wooden blocks. You can carve your own runes into wood chips or purchase a premade set from the market. To practice this technique, all you need to do is place the rune stones or blocks into a pouch and set the intention of the ritual. Once you've asked your question mindfully and attentively, pour out the rune stones and let them scatter. You will get a series of stones or blocks with runes. This can be interpreted with aid from a detailed guidebook, not only to understand the meanings of the runes but also what the position of each one means. Only then will you be able to completely interpret what the universe is trying to tell you through this divination method.

Angel Cards

Although angel cards are often confused with tarot cards or oracle cards, they're separate from both concepts. Angel cards are meant to draw on the energy of our angel guides to seek guidance from them. This type of divination tool is mainly used to find out more about one's future, finances, love life, and family matters. There are different variations of angel cards, so select the ones that draw you close to them the most. While tarot cards focus on the metaphysical meanings of life, angel cards approach angelic concepts and provide a different interpretation.

Start your practice by setting the intention for the process and bringing the deck of angel cards close to your body, placed near your heart. This will allow you to connect with your angel guides or spirits. When you're ready, draw a few cards and lay them out on the table. Examine the illustration and position of each of these cards to make an interpretation of the reading. Use a guidebook until you get the hang of each of the cards' meanings.

Astrology

An eminent divination technique, astrology has regained massive popularity over the past few years. Essentially, astrology relies on the position of the stars at a given moment and connects it with our specific persona. We can tune into nature and the universe through astrology to discover more about ourselves. The cosmos is constantly in motion, which can help connect our present state with the star's positions.

We can define astrology as the study of the relationship between celestial activity and events taking place on earth. Earthly events can include your career, relationships, finances, fortune, and wellness insights. Astrology uses the specific birth charts of each person to get a specific reading for them. This can then be interpreted more deeply to get guidance about all aspects of life. In parallel, birth charts tell a lot about a person, their past, and their probable future. Personal compatibility can also be determined using this method.

Numerology

Numerology is concerned with numbers, their combinations, and various mathematical symbols. This divination practice can help you tap into the underlying patterns of the universe and identify who you are deep within. One important aspect in the practice of numerology is your life-path number. This number is usually calculated using your date of birth and represents your present personality. This number highlights the specific traits and characteristics that are a big part of your life and will remain influential throughout your existence.

This divination technique ultimately looks at numbers to find the hidden meaning. Often, certain numbers present themselves to us again and again. These are not simply coincidences but, in fact, a pattern that the universe is asking us to identify. Another important aspect of numerology is our life number, which is associated with our birth date and intentions. Natal charts are also commonly used in numerology practices.

Tea Leaves

A less common divination tool used among psychics is tasseomancy, or the use of tea leaves to predict the near or far future. This technique requires specially made tea cups to help interpret the marks left behind from tea leaves.

To practice this method, first, brew fresh tea and drink it, but not completely. Make sure you leave a few drops behind. Move the cup in a circular motion and slowly drain the remaining liquid. However, ensure you don't drain the tea leaves with the liquid. Once you've done this, you'll begin to observe a pattern or shape forming inside the cup. Roughly sketch these images in your journal and interpret them with regard to the question at hand.

Divination tools are a great way to better connect with your spiritual energy and manifest the universe's energies to help guide you. However, we should always be mindful of how we use these tools. Understanding and learning different divination techniques allows you to comprehend how your spirit guides want to communicate with you. From there, you can further clear the communication path between yourself and the universal guides.

Nowadays, tarot cards are the most popularly used divination tool. This is followed by pendulum magic and the use of crystals. Each of these divination tools has multiple purposes, and as a psychic, you have both the skill and the ability to master these techniques and enhance your spiritual connection. Psychic practitioners also use other techniques like incense, essential oils, palmistry, and crystals to clear their chakras, enhance their vibrations, and strengthen their intuition. Ultimately, only you will determine which practice or practices resonate with you the most and help you achieve your goals as a psychic.

Chapter 6: Types of Spirits and Guides

Until now, you've had a chance to unlock and sharpen your psychic skills and learn what tools to use and how to protect yourself during psychic work. After this, you've probably become increasingly curious about spiritual communication and finding allies in the spiritual world. This chapter will introduce you to the spirits and guides you can ally yourself with. Some of these friendly beings will contact you on their own, while others need to be called on. The former can appear periodically or just once, depending on how and when you need them. Other spirits and guides may accompany you through your entire life. Either way, knowing who they are, how they can help you, and how they manifest themselves will help you establish a meaningful connection with them.

The one guide you'll always be able to count on is none other than your higher self.

https://www.pexels.com/photo/crop-female-future-teller-with-tarot-cards-on-table-4337135/

Ancestors

The most commonly appearing spirits and guides are the ancestors. These are the souls of people with whom you had a blood relationship, which makes contacting them easier. In most cases, you've never met them, although you might have heard about them from living relatives. Whether they lived twenty years before you or two hundred, the ancestral spirits have ascended to a higher plane from where they watch over you. Some may be waiting for reincarnation to acquire more spiritual wisdom and become more enlightened, while others remain in the abyss to help the younger generations. Since they're related to you, they might reach out to you if they feel you could use their help. However, in most cases, you'll need to contact them if you require their wisdom. Ancestors are known to send subtle yet clear messages, appearing in your dreams in their spiritual form. Or you may unexpectedly see or hear their name in certain situations. You can heed their wisdom for divination, spiritual healing, and any time you feel stuck in your life.

Departed Loved Ones

Like the ancient ancestors, recently departed loved ones may also become your spiritual guides. However, they might remain for a short period until you need them - or, in most cases, until they need you. These are people you knew personally, so more often than not, they'll need your help to move on or accept their role in the spiritual plane. That isn't to say that they can't help you in return. In fact, because you know them personally and vice versa, they'll be able to assist you more quickly and efficiently than ancestral spirits. For example, suppose you need guidance choosing the right career path. In that case, a recently departed soul may be more attuned to what you actually desire to fulfill your professional dreams. They can appear in dreams and visions, or you may hear their voice giving you the advice you need. They can also send you small signals, such as their favorite song, on the radio. You may also suddenly encounter or think about their favorite color, food, flower, or a personal object they once held dear.

Role Models

Even if you've had no close relationship or blood kinship with a person, they can still become your spiritual guide. Any person who influenced you in life can continue to do so after passing. This can be a role model, a person you admire for their qualities, someone with whom you share your life philosophy, or anyone else. Even famous people who inspire you can become spiritual guides. They may not appear to you personally, but they can send you small messages and advice if and when needed. You'll most likely need to contact them to gain their assistance, but if they're willing to help you, they'll make sure you receive their messages.

Ascended Masters

When someone reaches the highest spiritual level in their former life, they may remain in the spiritual plane to assist the living. These are the ascended masters, offering help to anyone who needs it, regardless of their cultural or religious background. They lived their lives gathering spiritual knowledge, which earned them a unique place in the spiritual world. While some of these souls may also be awaiting future reincarnation, most linger as supporting spirits, as they have much wisdom to share with the next generations. Being in an ascended form, they can access even more knowledge from the higher planes. A group of ascended masters can communicate amongst themselves, often working together to help multiple people simultaneously.

While you may encounter souls who were known to be famous spiritual masters during their lives, you may also meet one without realizing who they are at first. However, when they decide to share their knowledge, you'll be surprised to see how much they can teach you. Some masters choose their students and only work with mediums they feel they can trust to use their knowledge as they would. Others can be contacted for various purposes. Ascended masters can appear in their human form or as spiritual beings with auras. There is also a chance they might not materialize at all. Rather, they leave along signs that you'll pick up with your extrasensory gifts. They also have their unique energy, which is more empowering than the influence of other spiritual guides. Feel free to tap into it and use it as an anchor as you embark on the experiences they guide you toward.

The Higher Self

The one guide you'll always be able to count on is none other than your higher self. This is the being you're destined to become, and because of this, it will do everything it can to aid and advance your spiritual growth. They'll provide a gateway to information hidden in your unconscious mind. The best part about communicating with your higher self is that you won't even have to reach deep into the spiritual world to do it. You're not looking for a spirit version of yourself outside your body - instead, you're looking for a part that's inside you. If you want to reach out to your higher self, intuition is the only tool you need. They can help you separate the rational thoughts from the spiritual messages buried deep inside your soul. This can come in handy during divination, healing, and many other practices. There are numerous ways your higher self can manifest. For example, it may come as a sudden thought nudging you to look beyond the surface regarding a specific area of life. It may also be a gut feeling about a person or job you're considering applying for or a need to surround yourself with people who can provide you with wisdom and love.

Animals and Other Natural Guides

Most psychic beliefs hold that the entire living world is enveloped in the spirit, and all living beings have an essence. Therefore, it isn't surprising that when you venture into the spiritual world, you'll encounter several animal spirits ready to help you. Animal spirits and guides can be just as powerful as their human counterparts - they only communicate differently. Most often, they'll leave you subtle signs. You may see an animal appearing in your dreams a couple of times, in which case, they're trying to communicate with you because they have important news for you. There are different types of animal guides and spirits. Some will appear only for a short period when they're needed, and others will accompany you during a difficult stage in your life. Others will only show you how to encounter your permanent guide.

Some believe that plants may also have the ability to forward spiritual messages. Psychics who love connecting with nature or work in spiritual healing may get signals from herbs and other plants. Like animals, plants may also try to communicate by appearing around you or appearing as visions and in your dreams. They can also be called upon and asked to show specific ways for their uses.

Spirit Animals

Unlike animal guides that appear and disappear when their mission of helping you with a particular task is done, spirit animals are more loyal creatures. These are often the spiritual versions of a pet you've recently lost. They remain beside you to help you heal and allow you to move on. If they see that you still need their guidance after that, they may accompany you for the rest of your life. Spirit animals may also appear to people who haven't had any connection to them in life. An animal may appear to a child to teach them a lesson and remain by their side as the child grows into an adult. They can teach you valuable life lessons far more than any other human spirit can. Animals are driven by their instincts and are willing to listen to them - something people often forget how to do. Their advice can come in handy when you can't make a decision or have trouble discerning the true scope of a challenging situation. They can appear in pictures, movies, music, your dreams, or in the park if it's their natural habitat.

Deities

Depending on your religious beliefs, you may also have deities as spiritual guides. Some believe deities are the primordial spiritual ancestors, the source of all human souls. Other religions say that deities were once people themselves: like ascended masters, they've reached a level of spirituality in which they've gained divine status. After their final reincarnation, they've become spiritual guides ready to help people whenever needed. They typically appear in forms of energy, which is how you'll perceive them with your extrasensory gifts. If you feel a sudden burst of energy after praying to a deity, they let you know they're ready to guide you. They can aid you in your spiritual journey - especially if your goal is to reach a higher plane one day. They may also assist you during divination or when you have trouble discerning whether you're making the right decision or not.

Angels

Despite popular beliefs, angels don't only guide people with certain religious ideologies; they can assist anyone who needs their help. Also, you'll encounter different types of angels on your spiritual journeys as a medium. Angels typically send messages on their own and don't need to be contacted. However, you'll have to pay extra careful attention to your surroundings - even more so if you haven't worked with them before. You can receive messages in many forms, and while some signs will be loud and clear, others will be so subtle that if you aren't careful, you might overlook them. Fortunately, angels always carry meaningful messages. If you miss their signals at first, they'll likely try to reach you again and again until you start paying attention.

Guardian Angels

Like spirit animals, guardian angels are only linked to one person. As their names suggest, they are your personal guardians. However, you may have more than one angel guarding you throughout your life. While these beings devote their lives to helping one person, they know that not all of them can assist in everything. Just like humans, they have their own personalities and interests. As your personality grows and your interests change, you'll need help from angels more attuned to you during each particular phase. Whichever guardian angel you have by your side at any moment in time, if you need their help, they'll come to your aid. While most angels emerge without being called, guardian angels can also be summoned. Like deities, angels aren't likely to appear in their true form. Instead, they'll send signals through your dreams, visions, words, people, situations, or opportunities. They can be a source of wisdom for spiritual growth and divination. They'll also provide support and unconditional love when you need spiritual healing.

Archangels

Archangels are the most powerful figures in the angelic world. They've gathered wisdom in certain aspects of life, which makes them "experts" in these areas. Due to their status, they are less likely to appear without being summoned. When called, they'll leave their specific energy at your disposal. They can lend you great power, and you'll definitely feel the energy shift when they appear. Archangels can help many people at once, so they only appear in their energetic form. That said, they'll only appear if they feel that their energy is what you truly need. Otherwise, you may get another angel who'll only help you discover what you need. For example, if you need an angel with healing powers, you need to summon the strength of Archangel Raphael. If you want to reveal the truth or find a way to protect yourself from lies, Archangel Michael will be the angel to turn to.

Helper Angels

There are "lesser" angels who don't have a specific task yet, nor do they have immense power like archangels. Instead, they're looking out for all of humankind. These helper angels roam the divide between the worlds, waiting to see if anyone needs their assistance. Chances are, if it's the first time you're sending messages to the angelic world, it will reach one of these free-roaming angels first. When they receive a call for help, they'll see if they can be of aid or if they need to refer you to another guide. Helper angels can be most helpful in specific situations when you need a boost of spiritual assistance in your psychic work. For example, they'll provide that help when you want to find a way to befriend your colleagues at your new workplace. If they can't help, the helper angel will pass on your message to an archangel.

Light Beings

Spiritual guides can come from far beyond the worlds in our galaxy. They can also come from other galaxies and even be ancestral spirits. According to certain beliefs, the inhabitants of all galaxies are related to each other. They can also communicate in spiritual form. Just as souls can reincarnate in this world or any other galaxy, they can also be reborn in other galaxies. Souls you encounter from another universe are called *light beings*. Even if they live light-years away, they can share the wisdom of their ancestors and become unique guides. Because they aren't familiar with our world, they can offer a different perspective. It is often helpful when you want to see things with better clarity.

They may appear in the form of energy, a spark, a flicker of a star in the sky, a name of a new star written in the newspaper, or any other astrological or astronomical phenomenon. While not every medium is sensitive to their messages, if you receive them, feel free to take advantage of their knowledge.

Transitional Species

Depending on your religious and cultural background, you may also encounter spirits that belong to transitional species. Typically, these beings are part human and part animal or another creature. The most common guides among transitional beings are fairy-like creatures, mermaids, and centaurs. However, other magical beings like harpies, fauns, or sphinxes can also become spiritual guides. Some of these creatures live in the spiritual world, whereas others have a realm of their own. While not all of these are friendly, plenty of them can become your ally in times of need. Their human part helps you form a connection with them far more quickly than you would do with some animal guides. You will have an easier time communicating with them because they'll understand you better. However, and for the same reason, they'll often expect your help in return for theirs. They can protect you when you're in the spiritual world (or theirs) and prevent malicious transitional beings and spirits from crossing into our world. They can assist with spiritual healing. Most transitional species will appear in their true form - whether in your dreams, visions, or in pictures and symbols linked to them - and which you keep seeing all around you.

Universal Spiritual Energy

Some psychics don't hear, see, or sense signals from a particular spirit. This may be a transitional period, or you may never be able to rely on one guide. However, you may be able to tap into the universal spiritual energy. It doesn't matter whether you feel this energy emerging from nature or the universe itself. If you can tune into its frequency, you'll be able to sense how it permeates your senses and surrounds everything around you. It ties you to every other part of itself. This means it helps you access information without relying on a particular being. You'll always have access to this energy - you'll just have to reach for it. This is similar to how you connect to your higher self. Except, here, the wisdom comes from the outside. If you can't find your spiritual guide and can't access the spiritual wisdom you need through your subconscious either, the universal spiritual energy may be the best source to turn to. You may gain access to your guide through this energy, or you may continue relying on it if you still don't feel connected to a guide in the future. Even if you form a connection with a specific spirit, the universal spiritual energy can help deepen your bond.

Chapter 7: Methods of Spirit Communication

Continuing with the topic of spirits and guides, this chapter discusses the practical side of spiritual communication. In the following pages, you'll learn plenty of user-friendly methods and rituals for getting in touch with spirits and guides, from meditation to divination to journaling. You'll also receive valuable tips for honing your intuition and training yourself to become better at spiritual communication. Spiritual energy is on higher planes, so it may take some time and practice to achieve the desired results. That being said, when you start enjoying the fruits of your labor, all your efforts will be worth it.

Spiritual energy is on higher planes, so it may take some time and practice to achieve the desired results.

https://www.pexels.com/photo/assorted-tarot-cards-on-table-3088369/

Start Asking the Spirits

The best way to begin developing an ability for spiritual communication is to start asking the spirits. If you're at the dawn of your spiritual journey, your daily tasks may distract you from knowing that you have higher powers to rely on. By getting into the habit of asking, you're reminding yourself that you always have access to guidance - whether it comes from within you, your spiritual guide, a deity, or the universe itself. Besides, the more times you ask them for any form of assistance, the more gifts they'll bestow upon you.

To help you get started, consider how spirits and guides can help you achieve your goals. Make a list of 3-5 issues you need help with, and choose a being whom you want to ask for assistance. Ask one question at a time and wait for the answering message. When you get your answer, take your time to ponder it so you can resolve your issue successfully. After this, you can move on to asking the next question. Beginners should start with blood ancestors or recently passed loved ones, as they're typically the easiest to contact due to your shared relationship. If you've already established a relationship with a particular spiritual guide, you can ask them, too. Whether you prefer to ask the spirits after focusing on your question for a few minutes or do it within the scope of an elaborate ritual, make sure you're being polite and respectful. Present the issue as an offering, invite the spirit or guide to help, and express your gratitude for the assistance you might receive in advance. Making this a daily habit will enable you to establish a clear line of communication with your spiritual allies.

Ask for Specific Guides

Asking for specific guides will make it much easier to reach them. It will also help you avoid encountering unhelpful or malicious spirits and creatures. Consider what kind of guidance you need and who may help you with it. Be specific and think about who will offer the highest truth on that particular occasion, as this is the spirit you want to align yourself with. Don't overthink it - most of the time, you'll know who to call on instinctively. And if you truly need their help, they'll come. Once you've established who to call, you can send a message anytime. Generally speaking, it's best not to wait until the problem escalates. Instead, tackle it while you only need a little help. As a beginner, you may have trouble focusing on maintaining a connection for an extended period. This is only exacerbated by stress, so try to avoid it by seeking spiritual assistance as soon as you detect a problem. Better yet, don't wait for it to arise at all. Talk to all your guides regularly, and when they notice you have a problem, the one you need will reach out to you.

Look Out for Signs

Sometimes, spirits and guides will contact you on their own - especially if they have meaningful information to share with you or want to warn you about something or someone. Make sure to keep all your senses open for their signs. The same applies to situations where you're reaching out to them. While you wait for their response, you'll need to be vigilant and pay special attention to your environment. The simplest way to do this is to stop whatever you were doing for a few minutes from time to time and become more present. Empty your mind and explore what your senses tell you about your environment. This grounding helps slow your vibrations to align with the energetic signals the spirits send you, allowing you to notice them. Whether you'll hear, see, sense, or simply know you've received the wisdom depends on the scope of your abilities. Remember, it can appear everywhere around you, but it can also come from within you.

Align Your Energies with Mediation and Prayer

Whether you have trouble defining your problem or focusing on your intention, it can hinder your ability to reach out to your spiritual allies. A short meditation session can help you regain focus and discover what you need help with. It will also allow you to align your spiritual energy with the energy of the spirits and guides. Start by finding a tranquil space where you won't be distracted. Turn your focus away from your conscious thoughts so your mind isn't occupied with worries and to-do lists. Then, start focusing on your breath. Take a few deep breaths and feel how the air travels through your body. When you feel relaxed, visualize a warm, golden light enveloping you from all sides. Picture the guide you want to call on, and feel their energy meeting you through the light around you. Be positive and grateful for the energy that will now allow you to ask anything you want. Then, proceed to ask your question or seek assistance. Repeat this process for 5-20 minutes every day or whenever you feel disconnected from the spiritual energies.

Alternatively, you can say a prayer, with or without meditation. You can recite one before or after meditative exercises, or simply when sitting at your altar, or anywhere you get the chance to reflect on spiritual communication. Although it doesn't have to be a long prayer, don't forget to give thanks. You can say something like this:

"Thank you, my guide, for illuminating my path and showing me what to do regarding my health/work/relationship. I ask you to keep leading me in the right direction, and thank you for whatever blessing you may give, for I know I will need it for sure."

Build an Altar

While altars are traditionally associated with religious practice, you don't have to follow a specific belief system to build a dedicated sacred space. Altars are also ideal for spiritual practices because they allow you to focus your energy and intention on what you're doing. Even building a simple altar and decorating it with a few meaningful items can take your mind off other stressful tasks. An altar can be any flat surface you want to dedicate to your practice. How you set it up depends on its purpose. If you work with deities, you'll need to represent them by their symbols, favorite offerings, and color correspondences. If the purpose of the altar is to honor your ancestors, you can decorate it with their favorite items, food, drink, colors, photograph, or personal possession. To adorn an altar for spiritual guides and animal spirits, you'll have to get to know them first. That way, you can use items they cherish and find inviting enough to come to your side. You can use your altar to seek help, express your gratitude, meditate, journal, or engage in any other spiritual practice that allows you to reach higher planes.

Use Divination

As we've explored in a previous chapter, you can use several divination tools for spiritual communication. Tarot cards, Oracle cards, and Norse runes are just some of the most popular methods. Each offers a simple way to contact your guide and ask for an answer, assistance, alignment, or whatever you need to attain your future goals. The tools you use will serve as conductors for the messages flowing back and forth between you and your guides. If you've never used divination tools, you may want to try several of them to see which ones fit you best. You can make your inquiry as simple or as complex as you want. For starters, ask a simple question by holding one object in your hand (one card, rune, or another tool). After closing your eyes, shift your focus to the energy surrounding the object in your hands. Take a few deep breaths in the meantime to help you relax and ground yourself. Then, ask your guides or spirits for their assistance, and open your mind to the answers you'll receive.

Try Journaling

Writing to your spirit guides is another way to contact them. While you can simply write on a piece of paper, you may want to turn this into a regular habit. If so, get a journal for penning your thoughts and wishes regarding spiritual help. This practice will allow you to revisit them in the future and track your progress in sharpening your psychic abilities. If you want to use the journal to get in touch with your guides, you may want to start with an invitation and expression of gratitude, such as follows:

"Thank you, my guide, for revealing the wisdom you wanted me to have. I welcome you to come to me in these lines."

Then, take a deep breath and let your thoughts flow. Write them as they come, whether they're random ideas, visions, short or long stories, or anything you haven't thought of before. They may all contain a message your guide wants you to have. So don't second guess anything, and instead, just record them. Your guides may also choose to speak directly to you while you're in the process of writing. You should generally write in the first person; if you've suddenly switched to the second person, your guide may be writing these lines. Or your handwriting may change when they take over. After you're done, read over what you've written and try to interpret their message.

Another way to communicate with spirits through writing is dream journaling. Instead of writing down your thoughts during waking hours, you're recording your dreams. Recite a quick prayer of gratitude before going to bed and ask your question. Place your journal and a pen on your nightstand. That way, you can record the messages you've received in your dreams as soon as you wake up before they disappear from your conscious mind.

Hold Silent Gatherings

One of the best ways to honor a spiritual ally is to hold a silent gathering, usually dinner, for them. In some traditions, this is done as a family gathering to honor past ancestors. However, you can also do this to reach out to any spirit or guide by yourself. Choose a sacred space you've cleansed beforehand to ensure only positive energy surrounds you. Prepare the spirit's favorite meals and drinks and leave the place at the head of the table empty for them. Serve the meal to all participants (including the soul you've invited) and sit opposite them. When you've finished your meal, offer a thought to the spirit. This could be a few lines expressing gratitude, a question, or anything you may want to say to them at that moment. Do this silently, and leave the room in the same way.

Appreciate Your Guides

As we've seen, from time to time, you'll want to show appreciation for your guides and spirits. This will help you keep your relationship strong. Apart from thanking them for the blessings they send your way, you'll also want to give thanks for any opportunities and assignments that helped your spiritual development. You may find these challenging at times, but it's critical to let the spirits know you're grateful for them - and that they're welcome to send more wisdom your way.

Make an Offering

Whether you do it at your altar, during a gathering, or any other way, making an offering is a superb way to show appreciation toward a particular spirit or guide. Remember that the offering doesn't even have to be a physical item. Surrendering a piece of information about your problem works just as well. Your spiritual allies won't mind even if you do it to vent or give yourself a break. It's like getting to know a friend. They want to know how to help you, and you are giving them a tool to do so by offering something about yourself. They'll also be grateful because they know that your offering is a show of trust.

Ask the Spirits and Guides for Their Names

If you're working with your ancestors or the soul of a departed loved one, pet, or anyone you knew by name, you probably won't have trouble finding a connection with them. Names have an incredibly powerful effect on forging bonds between souls. Like you would when meeting a new person in the physical world, learning each other's names is often enough to break the ice and get the conversation going. However, if you don't know the name of the spirit or guide you're trying to call (or who is trying to reach you), everything becomes more challenging. If this happens, feel free to ask their names and offer yours in return. They may already know yours, but saying it will make it more likely that they reveal theirs, too. Focus on your intention, and ask for their names in your thoughts. The first name that comes to you is the name of the spirit who answered your query.

Additional Tips

Trusting your psychic ability is perhaps the most challenging task you'll ever face as a new medium. You'll need to fully believe that your gift will allow you to call on your guide and interpret their messages. So, if you have trouble with spiritual communication, you should look into yourself to see why. Do you trust your instincts, your gateway to your psychic gifts? If not, practice honing them through simple exercises until you become confident in your abilities. The more you practice this, the more frequently you'll be able to receive spiritual messages and allow them to guide you through the journey of life. Your gifts and the wisdom you receive can be helpful to others as well.

You'll also learn to trust your spiritual guide. While many psychics go above and beyond to make their guides trust them, they still have trouble returning the sentiment. If you doubt their ability to guide you, your bond will never be strong enough. Remember, spirits and guides possess a higher knowledge. They're aware of plans and fates you have no knowledge of, and the ones willing to become your allies are there to protect, guide, and love you. Don't try to control the situation by focusing on the outcome you think you want them to lead you toward. Let them decide, and you won't regret it.

Another tip to facilitate your spiritual communication session is to ground yourself afterward. Spiritual energy is empowering, but the energy shift you feel when receiving a message can be unsettling. It can prevent you from interpreting the information correctly and make you fearful of the next session. To avoid this, perform a quick grounding exercise after each session. You can do this by taking off your shoes and feeling the found with the soles of your feet, sitting on a rock in the park, or simply finding a patch of nature and taking in its stillness. Do anything that works as a reminder of your presence in this world and your human experiences.

Chapter 8: Journey into the Astral World

In this dedicated chapter, you'll learn everything you need to know about astral projection. You'll understand what the astral body and plane are and find out more about the idea behind astral projection. You'll discover various benefits of this practice, as well as some other ways in which you can achieve out-of-body experiences. Finally, you'll find a step-by-step guide on how to perform astral projection.

Everything that happens beyond our normal level of consciousness, including our dreams and out-of-body experiences, occurs in the astral body.

https://www.pexels.com/photo/man-love-people-woman-6014742/

What Is an Astral Body?

Yogic philosophers believe that we have three bodies (the physical, astral, and causal) that operate as the instruments of the soul. For starters, the astral body is considered the physical body's equivalent in the spiritual plane and isn't as prominent as the physical body.

Our **astral body** is subtler than the physical body and contains the "astral tubes" or "nadis," energy channels that carry the universal life force known as the prana. A person's mind and senses also lie in the astral body.

The **causal body** is the subtlest and can be found within the physical and astral bodies. It's the body that carries a person from their current life to their following reincarnation. This body also includes a record of a yogi's actions, experiences, and mental imprints in all plights of existence.

Our emotions and imagination are all channeled into the physical body from the astral body. The astral body is believed to detach from the physical one whenever we lose consciousness, sleep, or take any type of drugs or pain-relieving medications. That way, we don't feel any emotions or pain. The idea of the astral body entails that practitioners believe in the existence of the afterlife. This is because it is believed that our physical bodies are carried into the other realms via this vehicle after we die.

Everything that happens beyond our normal level of consciousness - including our dreams and out-of-body experiences - occurs in the astral body. This is why you must increase your awareness of this medium by meditating, partaking in Shamanic practices, or practicing any other method that can help you enter a trance state. Some yogis suggest that the astral body can appear as an aura floating around the physical body. Even though the astral body keeps changing colors, it's comparable to ether and is believed to be tied to the physical body's navel by a silver string.

What Is the Astral Plane?

Plato was the first to come up with the philosophy of the astral plane. He posited that planetary heavens exist in this realm and is home to the astral body. By the 19th century, the term astral plane was used by

Theosophists and neo-Rosicrucians.

The concept of the astral plane was expanded upon by oriental, medieval, esoteric, and classical philosophies, as well as other religions and belief systems. This plane is thought to be traversed by human souls before they're born and after they die. Angels, spirits, and other divine beings reside in this realm. Some people believe that the astral plane is where the spirits live permanently after they die. They believe it's where the soul reunites with God and associates it with heaven.

What Is Astral Projection?

Many ancient cultures have conducted this esoteric practice known as astral projection. Nowadays, yogis and other spiritualists believe it can help them enrich their spiritual practices. They also use it as a self-help tool. In reality, astral projection sounds a lot more complicated than it is. While some aspects of transcending your body are bound to be challenging, you can master the process thanks to dedication and practice.

Astral projection is an *intentional* out-of-body experience. These unique occurrences are mostly associated with lucid dreaming. Simply put, out-of-body experiences alter the brain's perception of your physical body. Your brain may be convinced that a part of your being is exiting your body. However, this is only because your brain's body schema at that moment is foreign - you, therefore, get the feeling that your consciousness is separated from your physical body for the duration of the experience.

Yogis who practice astral projection believe that the soul detaches from the body during an out-of-body experience. As such, it takes off to another realm of consciousness, which is essentially the astral plane. While science has not yet agreed that a person's soul can exist separately from the physical body, not all spiritual phenomena can be explained or supported by tangible facts. Many people think that out-of-body experiences are a way of proving that a soul exists. However, this level of consciousness is simply an alternative means for brain function.

You can expect to be in a dreamlike state when practicing astral projection; the only difference is that you'd still be conscious, lucid, and in full control of your actions and decisions. You can also achieve this level of consciousness through self-hypnosis or meditation. Once you access this state, you can use your mind to transcend your astral body to other planes, allowing you to explore your mental renditions of all dimensions, time, and space.

What You Can Do with Astral Projection

- **Experience Spiritual Growth.** You can expand your consciousness by practicing astral projection. It gives you the opportunity to visit the plane of the afterlife before death, offering validation for what comes after you die. It allows you to experience the continuous nature of our consciousness and souls.
- **Work On Personal Growth.** Out-of-body experiences can help you visualize your goals as they unfold. They also promote creative thinking in problem-solving. These experiences can help you in your professional life, too. Fiction writers can benefit from visualizing the plot and action in their stories. Astral projection requires you to train your imagination, which can benefit artists, designers, and performers. You can use these experiences to get clearer divination answers.
- **Enrich Your Learning Experiences.** Astral projection serves as an opportunity to grasp a deeper understanding of the world and embark on higher learning journeys. It's an opportunity to start observing the world with an inner vision so you can understand the mystery behind hidden realities. Out-of-body experiences can help you deeply explore the relationship between your physical body and other levels of consciousness and energetic fields. It also helps you understand the relationship between other planes and the physical world and that of our levels of consciousness and the surrounding energies. Astral projections can also help you discern the role of a person's emotions in any given interaction.
- **Understand Spiritual Immortality.** You can fully grasp the concept of spiritual continuity by insulating your consciousness and astral body from your physical body. You can also find out what it's like to experience numerous aspects of the physical world through an astral lens. You can use this experience to gather deeper insight into shamanic practice, divination methods, and other forms of magic. Many people seek out-of-

body experiences because they allow them to experience several emotions and activities like romance, intimacy, sex, and love from astral perspectives.

- **Try Time Travel**. Astral projection allows you to remember or even engage in first-time experiences of the past. You can read the Akashic records, which are a collection of all thoughts, feelings, words, actions, emotions, events, and intentions that have happened in the past, are happening right now and will happen in the future. You can seek answers to any questions you have from the Akashic records. Out-of-body experiences enable you to explore history as it was and discover your relationships in the previous reincarnation. You can embark on as many astral adventures as you want.
- **Learn to Help In the Inner Planes.** Those types of experiences teach you to spread goodwill, positivity, and peace in the inner planes. It also allows you to help and heal those who are ill, people who are dying, and souls who have just died. Practicing astral projection can teach you to diagnose health conditions and work with healing energies on psychological and physical levels. Out-of-body experiences supplement your physical vision with an astral point of view.
- **Contact Divine Beings**. Through astral projection, you can spiritually communicate with spirits, angels, spirit guides, souls that passed, and other divine entities. This practice increases your psychokinetic and clairvoyant abilities and allows you to determine where lost people, pets, documents, or belongings are located. You can see your chakras and certain thought forms, which is the process of manifesting your desires.
- **Experience Astral Travel.** Astral projection allows you to travel without moving your physical location through Earth and the world beyond. Whether you wish to see your friends or explore remote places, you can do it all via out-of-body experience. You can venture into the past and explore the future. You can see past your past and future reincarnations or selves. You can travel through space to see the planets, the moon, and even the astral plane. Astral projection can take you to places you'd otherwise never be able to access, such as the inside of an active volcano, the Earth's core, or the ocean's

depths.

Our consciousness is far more extensive than we think. We don't always realize that a part of ourselves is constantly encouraging us to channel conscious things out of ones that are currently unconscious to make more of ourselves. Now, what does it mean to be able to make something conscious out of what's already unconscious? How do we get in touch with this inner calling? We simply have to truly believe that we really are more than how we perceive ourselves - so we can consciously go beyond the limitations of who we are.

This way of thinking is the essence of the workings of astral projection and how you can use it to your benefit. All humans are a lot more than just physical entities. Our being is a lot more intricate and deeply layered than just a physical body, a soul, and a mind.

Other Out-of-Body Experiences

You can explore the power of consciousness over the physical world through self-hypnosis, hypnosis, and other types of meditation. Those practices are meant to induce certain physical sensations that can help us enter a higher level of trance. A trance state or altered level of consciousness is a dreamlike, semi-conscious state. Lucid dreaming is considered a form of astral projection because lucid dreamers are conscious during their sleep and have some control over their dreams.

There are five different altered levels of consciousness, ranging from very light trance to very deep trance. The first is a state that causes you to become more aware of your physical sensations, thoughts, and emotions, and can be achieved through mindful meditation. A very deep trance is characterized by the total loss of one's consciousness (like being in a coma or experiencing dreamless sleep). When conducting any type of spiritual work, such as astral projection, it's best to operate those two extremes. The second (light trance), third (medium trance), and fourth (deep trance) are generally the best-altered levels of consciousness to work with, as they yield the best results depending on your intentions.

Besides entering a trance state, you can use hypnosis to give rise to complex response patterns. By doing so, you can learn to control your pain, strengthen your immune system, or decrease tension in your body. This is how powerful your consciousness is - you can use it to induce any biological effect. Meditation, biofeedback, and hypnosis can all be used to encourage your physical body to alter some of its functions and even start new ones.

You can also change your brain function by detaching it from your physical being so it can operate independently. Our being is not limited to our physical body. Biology is merely a tool that facilitates spiritual growth and allows you to explore the physical realm.

How to Perform Astral Projection

Step One: Prepare Yourself

Experienced practitioners may be able to induce astral projection just by clearing their minds and lying in bed before visualizing their astral body exiting their physical being. If you're just starting, you can search for a guided online meditation to help you *ground yourself.* For this to work, you must be in a very calm state and release any expectations or attachments to a certain result. Don't attach yourself to the idea of having to project astrally, as this can create unnecessary tension and anxiety. Instead, you should feel relaxed and look forward to experiencing new sensations throughout the process.

Invariably, everyone's experience with astral projection will be different. You may come to realize unique things or discover that you feel comfortable using one method of astral projection over the other after a period of experimentation. That said, the basics of getting in touch with your astral body so you can access the astral plane are pretty much the same.

You can't do astral projection on-demand - there are specific steps you must follow first. Think of this as a prepping phase that allows you to tap into astral aspects of your consciousness.

It's always best to start by making meditation a regular part of your routine. It can be as simple as taking a couple of minutes at the start and end of your day for mental solitude if you don't already have a regular meditation routine. If you struggle to achieve mental clarity and peace on your own, you can experiment with guided meditation, crystals, incense, or meditation apps.

You can access a deeper trance state through self-hypnosis to connect with your astral body. Here's a brief guide on how to conduct self-hypnosis:

1. Change into comfortable clothing and find a quiet spot where you won't be interrupted.
2. Set your intention. In that case, your goal is astral projection.
3. Fixate your gaze on a focus point. You can light a candle and focus on its flame as a reference.
4. Draw your eyes shut and bring your awareness to your breathing. Shift your awareness to your breath every time your mind gets distracted. Notice any tension in your body and visualize it drifting away with your exhalations.
5. Visualize your idea of a happy place and remain there for a while.
6. Repeat a mantra that helps you ground yourself and feel calm.
7. Once you're completely calm, visualize your goal vividly. Imagine everything down to the smallest detail and engage all your senses.
8. Affirm your intention or goal.
9. When you're ready, prepare to exit your hypnotic state by picturing yourself inhaling energy from your surroundings and sending it back with each exhale. You feel lighter each time until your body returns to its normal state.
10. Count down from 10 and tell yourself that you'll open your eyes and feel energized once you reach 1.

Note: Some people prefer to use lucid dreaming as a tool to access an altered level of consciousness instead. This would be a good option if you already practice dream work.

Step Two: Get in Touch with Your Astral Body and the Astral Plane

As you're meditating, visualize your projecting self (imagine a nearly transparent version of you) leaving your physical body. You may not achieve the desired outcome the first few times, which is entirely normal. However, you'll eventually get there with thorough practice.

Step Three: Begin Astral Traveling

You're only ready to start astral traveling if you're confident in your ability to separate both your astral and physical bodies. You can test if you're all set by trying to observe your physical body from an etheric point of view.

Once you're prepared, you should think of a destination you want to visit or a goal you want to accomplish by being in the astral plane. You shouldn't allow yourself to meander around this plane with no clear intention.

Slowly bring yourself back to the present moment whenever you're ready. You should always cleanse your space after you're done astral projecting. Be careful not to leave any undesirable energies lingering around.

Now that you've read this chapter, you can use astral projection for spiritual growth, introspection, healing, and more. You'll be able to access the astral plane a lot more easily once you familiarize yourself with the process. Many seasoned yogis can connect with their astral selves and journey into the astral world by simply practicing meditation. Don't lose hope if you don't get there right away - and ... *trust the process.*

Chapter 9: Telepathy - Communicating without Words

This chapter explores the concept of telepathy in depth. Here, you'll come across a few real stories of how telepathic connections were used to save lives. You'll also find a step-by-step guide on sharpening your telepathic abilities and establishing a connection to send and receive messages.

We all have innate telepathic powers that we can channel.
https://www.pexels.com/photo/wood-man-love-people-6014745/

What Is Telepathy?

Face-to-face or phone call conversations, letters, e-mails, and text messages are among the first few things that come to mind when we think about communication. No one ever thinks about mental communication. If you're new to the world of spirituality and have never explored the concept of telepathy before, then images of magic tricks and superheroes probably cross your mind upon hearing the word "telepathy."

Believe it or not, you don't need a wand and a bunny in a hat to communicate with others mentally. No need to be a seasoned psychic, either. We all have innate telepathic powers that we can channel. While some people's telepathic gifts are quite prominent, others need to spend more time and energy to foster and manifest them more effectively. Our ability to connect with other people's consciousness is a generational ability passed down from our ancestors.

So, what is telepathy, really? Telepathy is often depicted as the ability to have a full-on, back-and-forth conversation with someone else. However, it involves sending or receiving emotions and thoughts to or from another person. It is one of the forms of ESP or extrasensory perception.

As you can infer, telepathy takes place from a distance. The two people don't have to be in the same place, and it doesn't require the involvement of other senses like touch, sight, or hearing. Telepathic activities can be broken down into numerous types. However, the following four are the most popular:

- **Communication:** Telepathic communication is a direct form of interaction with another person without having to speak to them.
- **Control:** This is the ability to control or influence a person's behaviors, actions, or thoughts.
- **Reading:** Telepathic reading is the power to sense or hear a person's thoughts.
- **Impressing:** This is the ability to ingrain a certain thought, image, or word into someone else's mind.

Telepathy is a power that extends beyond our basic level of consciousness. To fully understand this ability, you must get to know the inner workings of humans on a more profound level and be able to connect deeply with other people's consciousness.

This can be done if you think of everything inside your body as vibrating energies. Our bodies generate frequencies that can tune into the consciousness grids of others. If both energies align, a telepathic connection can be established. Once you get the hang of it, you'll find that this energetic alignment is as direct as any of the physical senses we use to communicate on a daily basis.

Twin Telepathy

Twin telepathy is a phenomenon we've seen on TV numerous times. There's a popular belief that twins can communicate without saying a word. Perhaps you've seen a set of twins always complete each other's sentences, or who can tell what the other is going to say or do next? Sometimes, this connection is so strong that an individual can tell whenever their twin is wounded, unwell, or sad. Much research has been conducted to explore the validity of twin telepathy.

A very popular story about a set of twins prevailed back in 2009. Gemma Houghton, who was 15 at the time, had saved her twin after she was sent a telepathic message telling her that her sister was in need of help. Houghton described the experience as a sixth sense. She was on her home's ground floor when she felt a sudden burst of anxiety. For some reason, she took this as a sign to go upstairs to check on her sister, somehow sensing that she was unwell. When she did, she found that Leanne, her twin, had lost consciousness. Gemma was able to pull her out of the bathtub, which was filled with water, and saved her with CPR. When she was taken to the hospital, the doctors said Leanne had suffered a seizure.

One of the several reasons why twins are thought to have natural telepathic connections is that they have identical energetic frequencies and grids of consciousness.

They were created, nurtured, born, and raised under the same conditions, which is why they have almost identical vibrational levels. They don't need to align themselves to each other's frequencies to connect - the step that requires the most effort already comes naturally to them.

Telepathic communication is still possible for those who don't have twins (or wish to connect with someone other than their twin). However, we'll need to work harder to tune into the targeted person's frequency. While the process can sound incredibly complex, you may be surprised to find that you already exhibit some signs of telepathic powers.

Signs You Have Telepathic Abilities

If you're mature enough to read and understand this book, you've likely undergone many life experiences. What you don't know is that many of these experiences are telepathic. You may think you know so little about telepathy - you've never tried to fine-tune this ability before. However, upon reading this section, you'll find yourself recalling numerous experiences, some going as far back as your childhood, flooding through your mind.

Your Intuition and Telepathic Abilities Are Always in Play

One experience I vividly remember from my childhood involved a woman (who I believe had ill intentions). When I was around 10, the school bus used to drop me off at a stop that was 5 minutes away from my home on foot. Although the walk sometimes felt exhausting after a long day at school, I mostly enjoyed it. It was the most peaceful time of my day, away from annoying schoolmates and my loud baby brother.

The night before a particularly long and tiring day, I dreamt that a woman in a red coat wanted to kidnap me. I used to have nightmares every now and then as a child. However, this dream felt strangely intense. It came with such vivid emotions that I couldn't shake them off the following morning.

I had forgotten about it by the time the bus dropped me off. I was feeling so sleepy that the walk home was rather burdensome. I remember tripping over right when I thought I couldn't wait to get home. Now, guess who suddenly appeared right over me? A lady in a red coat. She held her hand out to help me up and said, "Do you need a ride? Poor kid. You look very tired." I jumped up on my feet and sprinted home as fast as I could.

You're probably wondering what this has to do with telepathy. The answer can be broken down into two portions:

1. I was a child. Children give in to their instincts more easily and naturally than adults do. We think over and over before we act,

even when we feel an inexplicable pull toward a certain path. We're all familiar with the "should I follow my heart or my head?" dilemma. This is why children welcome their telepathic powers as they are. They don't spend much time thinking things over. Trusting our instincts allows us to align with the frequencies of others more easily. When we let loose, we can gain insight into what a person has in store for us.

2. It was a dream. Telepathy usually happens during our dreams. This is because when we are asleep, we enter a very deep trance state, which makes our brain waves vibrate at a frequency that makes them responsive to a large amount of information. Since all human events are recorded in the Akashic records, the dream I had about the lady in the red coat was already happening in real-time.

Other Signs You Have Telepathic Powers

Your Third-Eye Is Trying to Tell You Something

Do you usually get headaches around the center of your forehead? Perhaps you feel tension or tingling sensations around that area. If you do, then this is a sign that you may have telepathic powers. Sensations in the center of your forehead mean one of two things: either you're receiving telepathic energy, or your third-eye chakra is expanding. In any case, you shouldn't worry at all. Work on sharpening your telepathic abilities and opening your third eye; these odd sensations will decline over time.

You're Highly Empathetic

Empathy and telepathy are very closely related. While telepathy is the ability to read or influence other people's thoughts, empathy is the tendency to pick up on other people's feelings and deeply relate to them. Empaths mostly receive waves of energy and emotions rather than give them off. Telepathic individuals, however, can send and receive energies and messages. Honing your empathic abilities can allow you to develop them into telepathic ones.

You Feel Oddly Close to the Spiritual Realm

If you're reading this book, this is likely a sign that you may be telepathic. Not everyone feels compelled to explore the world of spirituality. That said, those who do are likely in possession of gifts.

Your consciousness already knows everything that you are. It realizes that you have gifts that you need to foster, even if you haven't fully realized so yourself. You should explore your telepathic abilities if you've always felt the inexplicable need to connect with your spirit guides or access the Akashic records. People who are truly aligned with the natural world are also typically gifted.

You're Quick to Tell When Someone Is Lying

Can you easily tell whenever someone is not being truthful or is only giving you half of the story? Telepathic individuals have a claircognizant aspect to their powers, namely, the ability to sense when someone is presenting inaccurate information.

You Receive Other People's Direct Thoughts

If you're clairaudient, you may also be unknowingly telepathic if you hear other people's thoughts or have a feeling that you just know what they're thinking; your chances of possessing telepathic powers are high. This sign, however, is mainly relevant to those who've worked on developing and refining their gift.

You Can Transmit Messages to Other People

Telepathy is two-way communication. Besides being able to hear what others are thinking, you should be able to transmit messages to them, influence their thoughts, or ingrain a particular word or thought in their minds. This ability is also relevant to experienced individuals.

Why Use Telepathy?

Possessing telepathic abilities sounds rather "cool." However, this gift is also incredibly beneficial. Often, we find ourselves at a loss for words. Do you ever feel like you want to say something but don't know how to say it? Perhaps you can't say it at all.

How often have you wished you could call your ex-partner and tell them everything in your heart? Whether you want to scream at them for hurting you or wish to tell them that you still love them deeply, it's not the right thing to do. Telepathy, in cases like these, can be a very handy tool.

Honing your telepathic skills can allow your higher self to deliver messages you can't express in the material world. This can pave the way for closure, forgiveness, and even deeper connections.

You may feel silly or anxious at first. Be that as it may, it helps to think of your telepathic abilities as a sixth sense that you're still getting the hang of. Say you were raised as a bilingual child, but for some reason, you stopped using your second language ever since you turned 5. Twenty years later, you won't be able to speak the language, but it won't sound completely foreign to you. You just need to familiarize yourself with it and slowly start remembering it.

Telepathy is a vehicle that can get you in touch with other people, animals, celestial bodies, and nature. The more you embrace your gifts, the more you'll pick up on the messages conveyed by your ancestors and spirit guides.

How to Hone Your Telepathic Powers

Like other psychic practices, establishing a telepathic link with another person is a skill that requires plenty of work and practice. You must approach the process with a systematic plan, which is why doing it on your own can be quite overwhelming. Fortunately, the following guide is a great starting point:

Practice Meditation Techniques

Practicing meditation can help you enter a light trance state to prepare yourself for telepathic endeavors. If you have a meditation practice that you feel comfortable doing, make sure to incorporate it into your daily routine. If not, you can experiment with various techniques until you find those that don't feel forced. Worrying about whether you're doing it right defies the whole purpose of meditation - clearing your mind. You can also look up guided meditation videos or podcasts if you wish. Aside from clearing your mind, meditation teaches you how to intentionally focus your mind. It also trains you to redirect your thoughts whenever unwanted ideas enter your brain.

Imagine that you're working on an important project. Whenever an idea comes to mind, someone barges into your office to ask you a question. You start to formulate an idea, but someone enters again, asking you to sign off on a document. Essentially, this is exactly what your experience with attempting a telepathic practice would be like if you fail to clear your mind beforehand.

Pinpoint Your Strength

Like every other endeavor, some people are more skilled in a certain area. When it comes to telepathy, some practitioners are stronger senders, while others are better receivers. Keep in mind that neither strength trumps the other. It depends on what you naturally gravitate toward, and you'll work with both skills either way. However, it helps to start working with what you're more skilled at. Once you master that skill, you can start working on the other one.

If you're wondering whether you're a stronger sender or receiver, ask yourself which of the following situations you are most likely to find yourself in:

1. You call a friend that you haven't contacted in a while just to hear them say, "I was just going to call you," or "you've been on my mind lately."
2. A person comes to mind just a few moments before they call you out of the blue.

If the first situation sounds more relevant, you're likely a receiver. You're more skilled at sending messages if it's the latter.

Try Receiving Messages

Each time you talk to someone, make a conscious effort to tune into their thoughts. Do your best to identify their thoughts, regardless of what they say. This will likely be received as a feeling - you may "just know" that this is what they're thinking about. If you wish, you can practice with someone you trust first. Ask them to think of any topic, so you can try to figure it out. Avoid working with someone who's doubtful about this entire process, as they may cause a vibrational block.

Try Sending Messages

Always remember that you can't decode a message unless you're consciously making an effort to receive one. You can strengthen this ability by practicing the "hello-goodbye" method each time you walk into any room. After you say hello to everyone the way you usually do, say "goodbye" rather than "hello" in your mind. Pay close attention to their facial reaction. Are they taken aback or surprised? If they appear to be confused, then they likely received your message.

Research Telepathic Exercises and Practice Them

Luckily, there are numerous telepathic exercises available online. Find a few and test them out. You can start with this exercise:

1. Find a trusted someone to practice with. Use any deck of cards that you wish to work with.
2. Ask the other person to stay in a different room. Make sure that neither of you can see the other.
3. Draw four random cards and arrange them in front of you. Keep them facing down so you can't read them.
4. Flip any card over and draw in deep breaths. Relax and focus on the image on the card and consciously send this mental image to your practice partner.
5. As the receiver, they should open themselves to the message and accept it. Once they identify it, they should send it back to the practice.
6. Switch roles so you can practice the receiver's role as well.

When performing this exercise, make sure to lean into your intuition. Don't second-guess yourself, and proceed as your instinct tells you.

Telepathy in Love

Establishing a telepathic connection with your partner is similar to establishing one with your twin. Those who fall in love and build profound connections with each other typically have similar vibrational frequencies.

In the winter of 2012, a middle-aged woman called Tracy Granger was driving on frozen roads. Tragically, her car crashed into a block of ice, which caused it to fall down a humungous mountain. She was left with severe fractures in numerous areas of her body, including her ribs and neck. Granger was unable to seek help and knew that no one would be able to find her.

As a last resort, she communicated telepathically with her husband, who immediately felt her need for help. A few hours later, Granger was found lying in the snow at the site of the accident. Even though she was severely injured, she recovered fully.

Now that you know everything about telepathy, you're ready to explore your abilities and start honing your skills. Remember that you already have all the tools you need to get in touch with consciousness to transmit and receive telepathic messages.

Chapter 10: Psychic Healing and Self-Care

As multi-dimensional beings, humans possess psychic abilities. These supernatural abilities come from the spirit that inhabits your body. Think about it - you are a physical being and have physical abilities and needs. You're also a spiritual being, so you have spiritual capabilities and needs. These abilities differ from one person to another. No matter how different these are, they still have the same form: energy. When you exercise these psychic abilities, you also extract energy. Naturally, the more fuel you use, the less you have.

As multi-dimensional beings, humans possess psychic abilities.
https://www.pexels.com/photo/healthy-man-people-woman-6944691/

If you've spent a lot of time using your psychic abilities, you may have felt a bit tired afterward. Not taking a break or some time out to feed your spirit will eventually drain you out. If you've felt like your energy has dimmed, then you may be interested in knowing when and how to self-care so you can avoid a spiritual burn-out. This final chapter suggests various ways you can practice self-care and psychically heal yourself and others.

Psychic Healing

In essence, spiritual healing is comparable to visiting a therapist or going to the dentist. It's simply a healing session where you or your healer will replace the negative with the positive. There are different reasons one should be spiritually healed; perhaps just a regular session where you nourish your soul or for protection if you feel spiritually attacked or drained. Although endless factors lead to a healing session, the reasons are not as important as the *symptoms.*

Recognizing the symptoms will lead you to the root of the issue - besides, the faster you point out the symptoms, the faster you will heal. If you're psychically drained, you'll most likely experience fluctuations in your intuition. Struggling with listening to your intuition is another telling sign. You may also feel like your empathy has been negatively affected. This can manifest as ambivalence about people, animals, plants, or anything you care about. Losing focus in meditation is also another sign that you're psychically drained. If you were spiritually attacked, your root and sacral chakra would be affected the most. That is to say, you'll most likely suffer from unexplainable fatigue and may struggle with feeling safe in your body or out in the world.

Now that you know what to look out for, it's time to explore different methods to help you overcome this psychic mishap. In this dedicated section, you'll learn about herbs, breathwork, and various methods that can help you overcome this hurdle.

Herbs

Herbs are versatile ingredients you can use to heal and protect yourself and others. Their incredible properties can be used in various ways. For example, you can start with simple exercises like saging your house. Since sage has cleansing properties, it can clear the negative energy that's occupying a place or shrouding a person's aura.

First and foremost, open your windows. It's vital to aerate the space so that the negative energy can exit it. Get a sage bundle or sage leaves and safely set it afire to sage your house, especially your bedroom. Make sure you leave the burning sage in the space where you spend the most time. If you're healing someone, then draw a circle around them with sage smoke. Envision the smoke ridding the negative energy and ask the person you're healing to do the same. Rosemary also has remarkable cleansing properties, so you can burn it next to the sage for a more potent effect. Here are other herbs with cleansing properties:

- Parsley
- Cilantro
- Peppermint
- Holy basil

Sometimes, the negative energies in our lives can manifest as disturbing dreams or nightmares. Luckily, some herbs ensure a good night's sleep and keep your bad dreams at bay. These notably include:

- Thyme
- Lavender
- Chamomile
- Bay laurel
- Juniper

These herbs can be used in a variety of ways. You can burn them and ask them to clear the negative energy that's been haunting you and protect you during your sleep. If you don't wish to burn them, place the herb of choice in a small bag and slide it underneath your pillow. Set your intentions with the herbs, then go to sleep as usual. You can apply these methods with a friend who's also been struggling with a similar issue. Simply hand them an herb bag and give them clear instructions on how to use it.

Aromatherapy

The practice of aromatherapy can help you heal while experiencing joyful and relaxing states of consciousness. You can use aromatherapy while meditating, sleeping, dancing, visualizing, or relaxing after a long day.

You can use a candle diffuser or an electric diffuser. If you don't have either of them, then create a simple makeshift diffuser. Boil water in a pot and put your essential oils in. Take the pot to your room of choice and enjoy the aromatic experience.

Below, you'll find several essential oils recipes for your inner and psychic healing. To ensure a successful outcome, repeat words of affirmation as you inhale the aromatic scents. Draft positive affirmations that align with your healing experience.

For example, suppose your goal is psychic healing. In that case, you can repeat phrases such as: "As I breathe in this air, I am spiritually healing" or "My spirit is healing from all that is negative; my spirit has regained its positive energy." Use these statements as inspiration to draft your own for optimal, personalized results.

Healing Essential Oils

Recipe 1:

- 180 ml water
- 2 drops of Peppermint
- 3 drops of Eucalyptus
- 3 drops of Lavender
- 3 drops of Lemon

Recipe 2:

- Empty spray bottle
- 20 drops of Orange
- 40 drops of Lavender
- 40 drops of Frankincense
- ⅓ cup of Honey
- ⅓ cup of Avocado oil
- ⅓ Castile soap

Recipe 3:

- 180 ml water
- 1 drop of German Chamomile
- 4 drops of Lavender

- 4 drops of Orange

Recipe 4:

- 180 ml water
- 2 drops of German Chamomile
- 4 drops of Cedarwood
- 4 drops of Lavender

Breathwork

Breathwork is a broad term that refers to mindful breathing exercises. It's so powerful that it can alter the mind, body, and soul states. According to recent scientific research, sustained breathwork can heal the nervous system and effectively decrease anxiety, anger, and depression while promoting relaxation and alertness in the body (Zaccaro et al., 2018).

Various types of breathwork have healing properties. Go over the list below and check in with yourself to see which ones you'd like to try first. That said, it's important to note that breathwork can be dangerous for people with heart issues and pregnant women, so use this method mindfully and carefully.

Mindful Breathing

Mindful breathing is effective technique spiritualists use all the time. It's also known as the breath focus technique. This type of breathwork revolves around words of affirmation and visualization. The images you'll see in your mind's eye, accompanied by affirmations and breathwork, can psychically heal you.

Instructions:

1. Lie down or sit in a meditative pose.
2. Observe your breathing rhythm.
3. Do not change it, simply go on with it.
4. Place your palms on your abdomen and take a deep breath (your abdomen should be moving with your breath).
5. Now, switch between your regular and deep breathing a few times.
6. Notice how both of them differ from the other.

7. Take two shallow breaths.
8. Now, take two deep ones.
9. Place your palms below your stomach and let your stomach relax.
10. Witness how it inflates and deflates with your breathing.
11. Now, sigh every time you exhale.
12. Begin your visualization journey. Picture yourself healing from the inside out, imagine yourself feeling content and relaxed, or whatever image brings you joy.
13. You can also start reciting your words of affirmation. For example: *"I am psychically healing. I am spiritually healed."*
14. As you inhale deeply, picture yourself inhaling healing air that cures your insides.
15. As you exhale, picture the negativity exiting your body.
16. When you're done, reflect on how you're feeling in the moment.

Belly Breathing

This method is known as diaphragmatic breathing. It's commonly used to treat PTSD, trauma, and insomnia. Traumatic experiences greatly affect you mentally, emotionally, spiritually, and physically. Trauma gets stored in the body, which affects your chakras and causes an imbalance in your spiritual well-being. Diaphragmatic breathing helps you release trauma from the body and gradually heal from it.

Instructions:

1. Sit on comfortable pillows or lie down on a soft surface, like a yoga mat.
2. Feel the tension in your shoulders and relax them.
3. Place the palm of your dominant hand on your chest.
4. Put the other palm on your stomach.
5. Inhale slowly through your nostrils and feel the air entering your body all the way down to your stomach.
6. Feel the air moving the hand on your stomach.
7. Contract your abdominal muscles.

8. Exhale through the mouth.
9. Apply pressure on your stomach and notice how it falls as you exhale.
10. As you inhale and exhale, try to keep the chest still.
11. The only organ that should be moving is your stomach.
12. Repeat this cycle as many times as needed for the best results.

Pranayama Breathwork: Alternate Nose Breathing

Pranayama breathwork is a yoga breathing exercise. Yogis use this method to cleanse the body of unwanted energies and refill it with new, refreshing ones. Alternate nose breathing is one of the exercises used in Pranayama breathwork. It also has healing powers and rids the body of anxiety and stress. Make sure you follow the method correctly for effective results.

Instructions:

1. Sit in a comfortable position.
2. Cross your legs.
3. Place your right hand on your nose and your left palm on your left knee.
4. Exhale.
5. Apply pressure with your right thumb on your right nostril.
6. Inhale through your right nostril.
7. Close your left nostril with your fingers.
8. Remove your thumb from the right nostril.
9. Inhale and exhale through the right nostril.
10. Apply pressure on your right nostril again.
11. Remove fingers from the left nostril.
12. Exhale.
13. The pattern is complete. You can do this as many times as you like.

Crystals

Crystals are an effective tool people use to heal themselves and others. Every stone has its distinct energy and frequencies, which vibrate with different parts of the human body.

As you may know, there are hundreds of chakras in the body. Think of them as little energetic portals that give out and store energy. There are seven main chakras among the other ones. These chakras form a vertical line from your pelvic bone to the center of your skull. This line is vital and governs your spiritual, physical, emotional, and mental well-being. For that reason, these chakras must be maintained and unblocked so that you can fully enjoy yourself.

Every chakra responds to certain crystals because they vibrate at identical frequencies. If you're looking to heal yourself using crystals. Identifying the problem is the first step. For instance, if you've been stuttering more than usual or if you find it difficult to speak your mind, it may be that your throat chakra is blocked. Once the problem is identified, you'll need to pick a throat chakra crystal that you feel connected to.

Building on the previous example, let's say that you picked sodalite. Start by cleansing your crystal with incense or soil. Charge it with energy from the sunlight or moonlight. Now, set your intentions. Speak to the stone and ask it what you need it to do for you. Finally, place the stone on your throat and feel its energy replenishing your throat chakra. Imagine that the crystal is replacing the negative energy with positive energy. Give a dull color to the energy you do not want and a more pigmented color to the energy you wish to bring in.

Here, you'll find a collection of stones that have the power to unblock the seven main chakras. You'll also learn how blocked chakras show up as different symptoms that you may have previously experienced.

Root Chakra

Symptoms of a blocked root chakra: feeling lost, feeling empty, and disconnected from yourself and others, heightened anxiety, feeding your insecurities with material things, and fear of the future and change.

- Bloodstone
- Hematite

- Tiger's Eye
- Red Jasper
- Garnet
- Black Obsidian
- Smoky Quartz
- Carnelian

Sacral Chakra

Symptoms of a blocked sacral chakra: disconnection from your sensual and sexual self, low libido, difficulty experiencing joy and pleasure, and lacking desire and motivation.

- Amber
- Orange Sapphire
- Orange Calcite
- Vanadinite
- Bumblebee Jasper
- Sunstone
- Fire Agate
- Imperial Topaz

Solar Plexus Chakra

Symptoms of a blocked solar plexus chakra: irritability, trust issues, adopting the victim mentality, irresponsible behavior, and low self-esteem.

- Pyrite
- Yellow Tourmaline
- Moonstone
- Lemon Quartz
- Golden Quartz
- Mookaite
- Fire Opal
- Yellow Smithsonite

Heart Chakra

Symptoms of a blocked heart chakra: difficulty letting go of the past, low empathy, poor boundaries, entertaining toxic relationships, paranoia, and anger issues.

- Malachite
- Aquamarine
- Fluorite
- Rose Quartz
- Green Calcite
- Amazonite
- Turquoise

Throat Chakra

Symptoms of a blocked throat chakra: social anxiety, struggling to speak your mind, poor communication, dishonesty, indecisiveness, and insensitivity.

- Sodalite
- Angelite
- Lapis Lazuli
- Azurite
- Danburite
- Blue Lace Agate
- Blue Chalcedony
- Kyanite

Third Eye Chakra

Symptoms of a blocked third eye chakra: entertaining judgmental thoughts, disconnection from dreams, spirits, and nature, poor intuition and gut feelings, and inactive imagination.

- Apophyllite
- Chiastolite
- Azeztulite
- Lepidolite

- Purple Fluorite
- Sugilite
- Chrysocolla
- Opal

Crown Chakra

Symptoms of a blocked crown chakra: lack of direction, inability to commit to goals, disconnection from spirituality, and inability to connect with self and others.

- Pearl
- Celestite
- Selenite
- Amethyst
- Labradorite
- Cacoxenite
- Seraphinite
- Dumortierite

Protection

Protecting yourself spiritually involves healing yourself psychically and caring for your spiritual self. If you've been spiritually attacked or if certain people or places lower your vibrations or darken your aura, you clearly need to protect yourself before stepping out of the house. Fortunately, there are many ways to spiritually protect yourself.

First and foremost, guard your house. When cleaning your house, add salt or sea salt to your water and soap to mop the floor. Salt is a powerful cleansing tool. Secondly, block your mirrors. Mirrors act like gateways or portals. Someone might be sending you malevolent energies through them. Clean your mirrors with a mixture of salt, water, and soap. Then, blow sage smoke toward the mirror. Draw a pentagram on the mirror with the smoke or with the salt water. Pentagrams will block negative energies from ever reaching you and polluting your space.

You can also set protective crystals around the house, such as black obsidian, selenite, or black tourmaline. These stones will shield you from negative energies. Alternatively, you can wear these stones as necklaces or pendants to protect yourself when meeting new people.

Lastly, envision a protective circle of light shielding you and protecting your aura from any unwanted energies. You can do this when you're at work, in the company of others, or when you feel uncomfortable around certain people or in unfamiliar environments.

Seek Guidance

Seeking spiritual guidance should be part of your self-care routine. While there are multiple ways to receive guidance from the spirit world, it's always best to receive it in a way that's most comfortable for you. For instance, if you're a tarot reader, then you may prefer seeking guidance through the cards.

Spiritually speaking, every being has been assigned a team of spirit guides before they entered the earth realm. This spirit team loves you unconditionally and assists you throughout your life. Naturally, people have sought guidance from this spirit team since time immemorial. If you wish to establish contact with them, then simply speak to them (you can refer to the chapter on spirit communication). Express your genuine gratitude for their existence in your life and ask them about anything that's occupying your mind. Ask them to give you signs so that your questions are answered.

There are also other ways to receive answers from your protectors. You can create a yes or no board and use a pendulum to understand what your spirits are asking you to do. You can also invite your spirit guides to a tarot session where they draw the cards that answer your questions.

Ultimately, healing is an essential process that elevates one's spiritual status and enhances their earthly experience. It's an ongoing process that never ends. In other words, you'll need to go through healing journeys as long as you're alive. The type of healing you need will differ from others because it is unique to you. This means checking in with yourself and seeing what your body, mind, and spirit need from you. Don't be tempted to compare your well-being to others, nor should you compare your healing journey with others' healing process. Everyone is different and will require various kinds of healing methods.

Whether you're a self-healer or you heal others, you must show empathy for yourself and others. In that regard, empathy is key to successful healing. This is why it's essential that you unblock your chakras and maintain their overall balance. You can do this by using crystals and these stones when healing others. Breathwork is yet another powerful tool that will help you heal yourself or others if you're a breathwork instructor.

Don't forget to have a spiritual self-care routine. This can take the form of house protection rituals and shielding yourself from unwanted energies. Seeking guidance is also another way you can spiritually take care of yourself. It can be done through contacting your spirit guides, conducting a tarot session, or any other psychic method that will offer you meaningful guidance.

Conclusion

As you've learned from this insightful book, psychic abilities rely on using one's extrasensory perception (ESP), also called sixth sense. This sense is tied closely to intuition, meaning a person with highly developed psychic skills has an intrinsic ability to pick up supernatural signals. Tapping into your intuition is another key step for awakening any latent psychic ability you may possess. The tips included in the opening chapter can teach you which signs you should pay attention to when trying to discover your skills. However, the only sure way to know you're on the right track is by listening to your gut feelings.

Among the most common psychic abilities one might discover in themselves are the clairs. These skills provide the pillars for psychic powers, and each clair has a unique contribution to their host medium on their own. Clairvoyance allows you to receive messages in visions, while clairaudience is the ability to hear spiritual messages. Likewise, clairsentience enables the medium to receive information through different sensations in their body, whereas claircognizance is a unique ability that comes with sudden knowledge without the receiver being aware of where or what form the message has come from.

While some of the messages may only confirm the knowledge you already possess in your subconscious, revealing them comes through your psychic abilities. To receive them, you must reach into the abyss, for which you'll need protection. Whether you're a beginner or an experienced medium, you'll never know what kind of unwanted or harmful forces you may find yourself against when trying to communicate through spiritual messages. Fortunately, there are effective ways to protect yourself against them and cleanse yourself, your space, and others from their negative influences. As it happens, the same applies to divinatory practices. While physics rarely uses tools for gazing into the future, they're helpful if you need future-related information from the spiritual world. Make sure these tools are properly cleansed and maintained as well.

Once you've discovered and begun to sharpen your psychic power and learned which tools can enhance it, you can move on to explore the different types of spirits and guides. Not all spirits you encounter during spirit communication will be friendly. Others may not be interested in working with you. For that reason, knowing how to distinguish between the spirits will allow you to choose your allies more carefully and establish a secure line of communication with them. There are several ways to communicate with spirits and guides; the one you should use depends on your intentions and skills. Certain guides or spirits may also have distinct preferences toward a form of communication, and you'll need to respect these.

Another psychic skill we've explored in this book is astral projection. This ability allows practitioners to use their astral body for journeying to the astral world. Practitioners may use several methods to have an out-of-body experience and step onto the astral plane, where it's easier for them to communicate. Telepaths, on the other hand, can communicate with living people using only their minds.

Last but not least, you've learned that using your powers can take a toll on your health. Other times, you'll be affected by negative energies despite your best efforts to prevent this. Either way, you'll need to be ready to heal yourself if and whenever needed. Implementing simple psychic self-care techniques into your daily routine will help you keep your mental and physical health in check and enable you to grow into an accomplished medium.

Here's another book by Silvia Hill that you might like

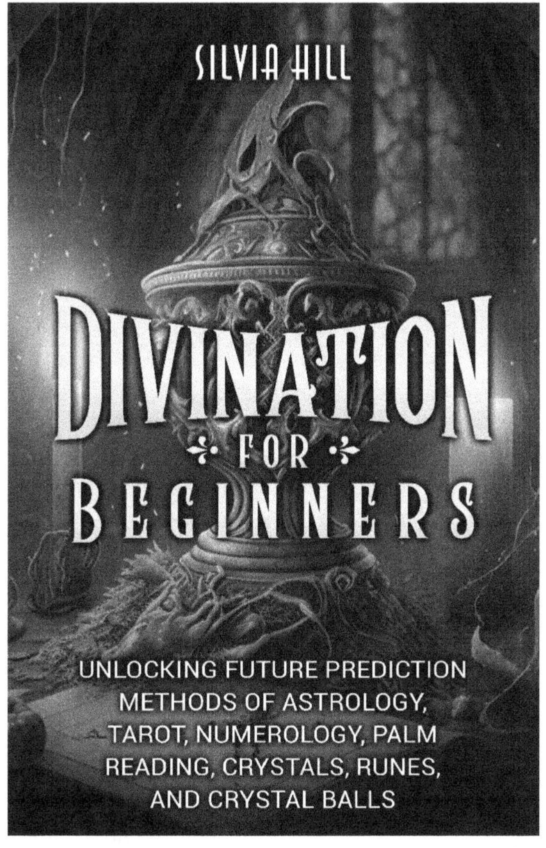

Free Bonus from Silvia Hill available for limited time

Hi Spirituality Lovers!

My name is Silvia Hill, and first off, I want to THANK YOU for reading my book.

Now you have a chance to join my exclusive spirituality email list so you can get the ebooks below for free as well as the potential to get more spirituality ebooks for free! Simply click the link below to join.

P.S. Remember that it's 100% free to join the list.

~~$27~~ **FREE BONUSES**

- 9 Types of Spirit Guides and How to Connect to Them
- How to Develop Your Intuition: 7 Secrets for Psychic Development and Tarot Reading
- Tarot Reading Secrets for Love, Career, and General Messages

Access your free bonuses here

https://livetolearn.lpages.co/psychic-abilities-paperbck/

References

Kelly, A. (2018, July 2). Am I Psychic? How to Tap Into Your Own Psychic Abilities. Allure. https://www.allure.com/story/am-i-psychic-how-to-tap-into-psychic-abilities

Miller, A. (2022, June 13). Am I Psychic? How to Know if You're Psychic - A Step-by-Step Guide to Psychic Abilities. Bellingham Herald. https://www.bellinghamherald.com/health-wellness/article262457037.html

Bailey, A. (2021, December 7). 10 surprising signs that you might be psychic. Bodyandsoul.com.au. https://www.bodyandsoul.com.au/mind-body/10-surprising-signs-that-you-might-be-psychic/news-story/7220ada2fd93f329915bbaa529a78eb6

Belfast, L. (2020, June 24). How to tell if you have psychic abilities. Lovebelfast. https://lovebelfast.co.uk/how-to-tell-if-you-have-psychic-abilities/

Coughlin, S. (2017, January 20). 14 real-life psychic moments from reddit. Yahoo Life.

Cytowic, R. E., & Wood, F. B. (1982). Synesthesia. Brain and Cognition, 1(1), 36–49. https://doi.org/10.1016/0278-2626(82)90005-7

Extra-Sensory Perception (ESP), sixth sense, or intuition unlocked. (2014, November 2). WisdomTimes. https://www.wisdomtimes.com/blog/extra-sensory-perception-esp-sixth-sense-intuition-can-unlocked/

Gut feelings: What they really are & how to know if you can trust them. (2021, February 26). Mindbodygreen. https://www.mindbodygreen.com/articles/gut-feelings-what-they-really-are-when-to-trust-them

Holland, K. (2022, January 5). What is an aura? 16 FAQs about seeing auras, colors, layers, and more. Healthline. https://www.healthline.com/health/what-is-an-aura

Jackson, L. L. (2016, January 11). 4 signs you might be psychic. Oprah.com. https://www.oprah.com/inspiration/psychic-abilities

Kelly, A. (2018, July 2). Am I psychic? How to tap into your own psychic abilities. Allure. https://www.allure.com/story/am-i-psychic-how-to-tap-into-psychic-abilities

Miller, S. G. (2016, September 22). A sixth sense? It's in your genes. Live Science. https://www.livescience.com/56223-sixth-sense-genes.html

Newswire, P. R. (2021, October 8). The true story of a modern psychic - clairvoyant medium Bernadette Gold reveals how she embraced her spiritual gifts in new memoir: "the crooked path to a charmed life." Yahoo Finance.

Raypole, C. (2020, March 30). What causes déjà vu? Common theories, symptoms to watch for, and more. Healthline. https://www.healthline.com/health/mental-health/what-causes-deja-vu

Sogani, G. (2020, October 3). Psychic abilities: Do humans possess them? Wondrium Daily. https://www.wondriumdaily.com/psychic-abilities-do-humans-possess-them/

Teale, J. C., & Oâ€TMConnor, A. R. (2015). What is DÃ©jÃ vu? Frontiers for Young Minds, 3. https://doi.org/10.3389/frym.2015.00001

Theodora Blanchfield, A. (2022, May 31). What is déjà vu and why do we experience It? Verywell Mind. https://www.verywellmind.com/what-is-deja-vu-why-do-we-experience-it-5272526

WebDev, I. E. T. (1995, November 28). "psychic spying" research produces credible evidence. UC Davis. https://www.ucdavis.edu/news/psychic-spying-research-produces-credible-evidence

What IS an aura? (and how can you see yours?). (2016, June 10). Mindbodygreen. https://www.mindbodygreen.com/articles/what-is-an-aura

What is it like to have psychic abilities? (n.d.). Quora. https://www.quora.com/What-is-it-like-to-have-psychic-abilities

Childs, G. J. (2003). Rudolf Steiner: His life and work (2nd ed.). Floris Books.

How to use your intuition like A professional psychic. (2017, June 13). Mindbodygreen. https://www.mindbodygreen.com/articles/the-4-types-of-intuition-and-how-to-tap-into-each

Reader, C. (2021, February 22). How to tell if you have clairaudience: 8+ clairaudience signs, abilities, and more. Chicago Reader. https://chicagoreader.com/reader-partners/how-to-tell-if-you-have-clairaudience-8-clairaudience-signs-abilities-and-more/

Sixth Sense Abcderium. (n.d.). Sixthsensereader.org https://sixthsensereader.org/about-the-book/abcderium-index/clairaudience/

Steiner, R., & Bamford, C. (2002). What is Anthroposophy?: Three

Perspectives on Self-Knowledge (M. Spiegler, Trans.). SteinerBooks.

Clairsentience: A somatic approach to intuition. (2016, June 17). Strozzi Institute | Embodied Transformation; Strozzi Institute. https://strozziinstitute.com/clairsentience-a-somatic-approach-to-intuition/

Cotroneo, H. (n.d.). The College of Psychic Studies : Workshops : Psychic and mediumship : The psychic tasting and smelling clairgustance and clairolfaction. The College of Psychic Studies. https://www.collegeofpsychicstudies.co.uk/workshops/psychic-and-mediumship/the-psychic-tasting-and-smelling-clairgustance-and-clairolfaction/

Garis, M. G. (2020, July 28). How to use each of the 4 'Clair' senses to receive information psychically. Well+Good. https://www.wellandgood.com/psychic-clair-senses/

Wahbeh, H., Yount, G., Vieten, C., Radin, D., & Delorme, A. (2019). Measuring extraordinary experiences and beliefs: A validation and reliability study. F1000Research, 8, 1741. https://doi.org/10.12688/f1000research.20409.3

Coughlin, S. (2018, August 14). 18 items that will ward off any bad vibes. Refinery29.com; Refinery29. https://www.refinery29.com/en-us/negative-energy-clearing-bad-vibes

Phillips, F. (2020, November 24). How to create a personal energy shield for protection. The Good Space. https://www.findyourgoodspace.com/blog/how-to-create-personal-energy-shield-for-protection

Aletheia. (2017, December 18). How to use a dowsing pendulum for divination - beginner's guide. LonerWolf. https://lonerwolf.com/dowsing-pendulum/

Brown, M. (2021, August 11). What is astrology? A beginners' guide to the language of the sky. InStyle. https://www.instyle.com/lifestyle/astrology/what-is-astrology

Colosimo, N. (2020, March 30). Tools for divination and developing psychic awareness. The Psychic School. https://psychicschool.com/tools-for-divination-and-developing-psychic-awareness/

Davis, F. (2021, October 13). 15 divination tools to spark your psychic abilities. Cosmic Cuts. https://cosmiccuts.com/blogs/healing-stones-blog/divination-tools

www.ingramcontent.com/pod-product-compliance
Lightning Source LLC
Chambersburg PA
CBHW060622310726
48982CB00003B/638

* 9 7 9 8 8 8 7 6 5 1 3 1 6 *